MW00425487

THE DRUM LIF

QUICK FIXES, HACKS, AND TIPS OF THE TRADE

BY PETER ERSKINE & DAVE BLACK

Alfred Music
P.O. Box 10003
Van Nuys, CA 91410-0003
alfred.com

ISBN-10: 1-4706-3899-1
ISBN-13: 978-1-4706-3899-3

Cover Illustration: Nick Beecher

CONTENTS

FOREWORD

Why drumset tips and tricks?

Fifty years of working as a professional drummer, for one. Collaborating with the best-selling author and drumming pedagogy expert Dave Black, for two. "Hacks," or unconventional pieces of advice, are a popular, effective way to deliver bite-sized bits of information distilled from a combined-years-of-experience totaling nearly 100 years (just a few years less than the age of the drumset), for three. And, four, why not?

While some of what we've collected here can be found in other books, we wanted to compile as much of that useful information as possible into one resource, and include additional information that didn't seem to fit into the standard drum book norm where basic technique, independence, styles, and so on, are discussed.

The additional info is, in other words, the really fun stuff.

Included throughout the book are incredibly practical, yet off-beat solutions to just about any drumming situation you will most likely encounter, whether you're a working pro, a student, or a weekend drumming warrior who simply plays the drums for the fun of it.

Whatever your musical preference or style, and whatever your level of drumming experience or expertise, we promise that you'll find answers to questions you've asked yourself before, or answers to questions that you didn't even know existed!

(Note: First-person comments in the book are provided by Peter.)

Herein we present *The Drummer's Lifeline.*

Peter Erskine & Dave Black
Los Angeles, 2017

PROBLEM: How do I play better?

TIP: *Listen to the music, and play what you'd like to hear...not what your hands know, but what your ears and heart tell you to play. It's really that simple.*

RULE: No licks! Compose when you play. Use your imagination, but always play for the song.

Job number one is for the drummer to provide rhythmic information to the band, and to play in a way that makes all the other musicians play their best. Within these duties, there is an infinite number of choices we can make (orchestration on the kit, the "temperature" and density of the beat, and so on). Add to that the often complicating factor or feeling of playing to someone else's expectations, ego satisfaction, audience response, and so on—this is when the muscles begin to take over the musical mind. The simplest solution? Just play what you'd like to hear, not necessarily what you'd like to *play*. Those can be two very different things. Experience brings the hearing and the playing process together as one.

PROBLEM: How do you pick up a pair of brushes resting atop a drumhead without making any noise?

You'd be surprised how often most drummers make noise when they simply grab or lift their brushes off the surface of the drumhead (especially during any quiet part of a tune, or during a "live" or studio performance). So, what do we do?

TRICK: In general, it's a good idea to get into the habit of placing your brushes on the top surface of the snare head, with a small portion of the handle hanging over the edge of the drum:

Simply place your open hands directly above the brushes.

Then quickly (and simultaneously) move your hands downwards onto the end of the brush handles, so the brushes will "see-saw" off the drumhead surface and silently up into the air.

Just grab the rest of the brush handle, and you're good to go. Make a good noise when you drum; never try to make an unwanted noise!

PROBLEM: My floor tom is ringing too long.

TRICK: Remove one of the three floor-tom legs, turn it upside down, and insert the upside-down leg into the mounted holder (*see photo below*). Now, instead of three rubber-tipped feet, your drum will have two rubber-tipped feet and one bare-metal "foot." And, presto change-o, your floor tom's sustain should be musically shortened or curtailed. A less drastic approach might be to remove one or more of your tom legs' rubber feet. We can thank drumming great and studio legend Jim Keltner for this bit of advice.

Recording studios are where this problem often pops up, because each studio drum room will have different ceiling heights, angles, and materials, all of which can affect the way our drums ring and sound. Floor toms seem to be the most susceptible to such unwelcome change.

ALTERNATE TRICK: Experiment with the relative tuning pitches between the top and bottom heads of the drum, and/or slightly de-tune one

or the other head. You can also try dampening the head with some sort of mute, such as a specially formulated gel for drums, gaffer's tape (with tissue), etc. However, remember that most external dampening solutions will deaden the head and change the nature of the stick's attack, thus changing the very nature of that one drum in your kit.

FUN HACK: If you forget to bring your floor-tom legs to a rehearsal or gig, you can always use drumsticks in place of the legs.

PROBLEM: Eyes closed

TIP: *Practice playing with your eyes open. Look at the source of the music, and do not close your eyes or stare off into space (usually off to the drummer's left...somewhere). Connect. We're trying to have a conversation up here.*

QUESTION: How do I keep my eyes on the conductor, as well as on the snare drum or tom I'm about to play?

ANSWER: Quietly (*silently*) place your sticks upon the playing surface in anticipation of playing. You will be in position and know exactly where your sticks are in relation to the playing surface. Trust us—this is a bigger deal than you might think.

QUESTION: Heels up, or heels down?

ANSWER: Both!

The short explanation is that you'll experience better control on both pedals when you master the art of playing the hi-hat and bass drum with your heels down. This method is certainly preferable when playing at soft- to medium-dynamic levels. Louder strokes invite (or demand) the use of the leg, so use heel "up" for additional weight and power. Multiple strokes on the bass drum are often best accomplished by playing heel up and gliding the foot frontwards on the pedal board in a tap-dancing motion. Practice makes perfect!

RELATED QUESTION: Shoes or no shoes?

ANSWER: Shoes.

Next question...

QUESTION: How wild (wacky, off-beat, signature) should I make my fills before the rest of the band comes in with a written figure?

ANSWER: The sky's the limit with musical possibilities and options when it comes to drum fills, but here's something to always keep in mind. Your fellow musicians are counting on you (and, literally, counting) to make their entrance following your set-up or fill, and they're doing this while readying/steadying their embouchure (lips on mouthpieces, etc.), and preparing to take a breath, etc. A drum fill that shakes the very foundation of their sense of well-being could result in a disastrous performance. You must know the music *and* your peers in the ensemble. Don Lamond made a living from playing some really off-the-wall drum breaks (check out Bobby Darin's "Beyond the Sea" recording), but his peers knew what to expect when Don was playing the drums. Plus, he always came out "right." You might want to practice such groundbreaking breaks with a metronome and record the results. If the break is confusing to you when you listen to it, imagine how it might be for others to comprehend.

QUESTION: I want to add rivets to my cymbal…where should they go?

ANSWER: First, a suggestion regarding *how many* rivets to add to your cymbal—I've found that *three* rivets seem to work wonders on most cymbals, and I like to position these in a cluster, approximately one inch between them. This row of rivets is best-situated at 1.5–2 inches from the edge of the cymbal, and may follow the slight radial curve of the groove. Do not drill these three holes randomly! Since most every cymbal has a heavy side—i.e., the side of the cymbal that normally comes to rest closest to you—you will want to determine the cymbal's heavy side and then place your rivets anywhere but there. In other words, you don't want to have the distraction of having to avoid hitting the rivets while playing.

Now that we have your attention, let's talk about some of the basics.

CHOOSING DRUMSTICKS, BRUSHES, MALLETS, AND BASS DRUM BEATERS

Although a lot of information regarding stick, head, and beater selection can be found on the Internet, we wanted to include the following information/commentary based on our own experiences. In other words, don't believe everything you read on the Internet.

Drumsticks

A drumstick needs to feel good in your hand. It's the connection between you and your instrument. Drumsticks are most often made of wood (usually hickory, maple, or oak). Plastic, fiberglass, and metal have been used as well, but most drummers use wood sticks, and we recommend you do as well.

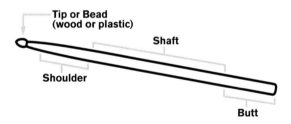

1. Drumsticks come in a variety of sizes and shapes, designed for different sounds and/or applications. A stick with a small tip is articulate, whereas one with a larger, rounder tip produces a broad, full sound. Too large of a tip usually results in a lousy cymbal sound.

2. Sticks are available with either a wood or nylon tip. Those with nylon tips are designed to produce a more articulate sound on the cymbals. When used on a drum, however, they sound almost identical to a wood-tipped stick.

3. "A" model sticks (originally designed for jazz playing) are smaller than "B" model sticks (designed for heavier use in jazz or concert bands), which are smaller than "S" model sticks (intended for street or marching use), which are smaller than "DC" sticks (designed for drum-corps use).

4. For beginning snare drummers, we recommend a "2B" or "5B" model stick. For those playing in a jazz or concert band setting, a "5A" or "5B" drumstick is a good standard beginner stick. For those playing in a rock or heavy metal band, etc., a larger pair of sticks may be necessary. Whatever your choice, you should always carry multiple pairs in the event they break, get lost, or are dropped.

5. When purchasing sticks, we recommend that you check them carefully to make sure you're buying a matched pair. The following guidelines will help you make that determination:

a. Visually inspect each stick for obvious flaws.

b. Tap each stick on a hard surface, and listen for an even match. Sticks that produce a high pitch are most likely made of dense wood, which is excellent for both sound and response.

> **TIP:** *One of the best ways to check stick pitch is to simply drop them one at a time on a hard surface! Holding them in any way while checking may well alter the pitch.*

c. Check to make sure the sticks are not warped by rolling each one on a hard, flat surface. Those that are warped should be set aside or discarded.

Some manufacturers take great care to pair their sticks as close to perfect as possible. Warpage or density issues are quite rare.

TIP: *If a stick sounds fine on your cymbals, it will most likely be fine for your drums.*

TIP: *Experiment with using different sticks, especially in different musical settings. The variety of stick tips and/or weights available can make a pretty big difference in terms of both sound and execution.*

QUESTION: Are weighted drumsticks good or bad?

ANSWER: Bad!

Brushes

Because brushes produce the second most-requested sound, every drummer should carry at least one pair. Brushes can be made of wire or nylon, be retractable or non-retractable, and have handles made of wood, plastic, or rubber-coated metal. Like sticks, they come in a variety of weights and styles.

QUESTION: Which brush do you use?

ANSWER: I prefer telescoping wire brushes with a rubber-coated handle, such as the Vic Firth Heritage Model.

Remember that the main purpose of playing with brushes is to *sweep* and add *texture* to the sound of any drum, particularly the snare drum. Use dead sticking to maximize the amount of contact time between the brush and the drum with every stroke. Brushes are not drumsticks.

You'll really want to choose your brush-on-cymbal moments very carefully, as there's no reason to play them if they can't be heard, right?

Meanwhile, play something like a simple four-stroke fill (with a right-hand start and alternating sticking) that leads to the bass drum. The key to playing this is to open it up, not speed it up!

TIP: *You can always play slower than you think you need to when playing single strokes with brushes (I'm not talking about time patterns, where sweeping motions are involved). The more "open" you play, the better it sounds. If it's too tight and rushed, your brush playing will sound like a burp. Practice this on the snare drum with the snares off, as well as on the floor tom. Resist the instinct to play your brush patterns faster…slower is better, no matter the tempo.*

What you will want to do fast is switch from brushes to sticks (and vice versa) as the music demands. To do this, I place my brushes on the floor tom's rim (closest to me), which allows me to still be able to play the floor tom. If the brushes are resting on the floor tom's head, I've taken that drum out of commission. You paid a lot for that drum, so use it!

BRUSH SPECIAL EFFECT #1: While holding the brush about an inch above the head, slap the shaft on the rim of the snare drum so that the force causes the bristles to strike the drum and bounce. This will create a vibrating effect. **NOTE:** This may label you as the drummer who likes to use a cheap brush effect. Use it sparingly, if at all.

BRUSH SPECIAL EFFECT #2: Lay one brush down on the snare head, and roll it back and forth with the palm of your hand. This will create a flapping sound that can be manipulated to create additional sounds. **WARNING:** This effect might make you eligible for the "Hot Dog Drummer Hall of Fame." I like it when Ed Thigpen or Jeff Hamilton has done this, but otherwise it's off limits for me.

BRUSH SPECIAL EFFECT #3: I find this one more useful and palatable …move either brush side to side on the drumhead out of tempo, simulating the sound of the wind (or, when moving the brushes slowly and in more of a circular pattern, something akin to the rustling of bed sheets…); moving both brushes side to side rapidly conjures up the image of leaves being tossed about by the wind…if you're into that sort of thing…I am.

GENERAL ADVICE: *Hear what it is you want to hear when you play. If you visualize it in your head and ears, it will become much easier.*

QUESTION: When playing with brushes, how can I reduce the harsh/raspy sound of a new drumhead?

ANSWER: Carry a small piece of light-grade sandpaper in your stick bag so you can remove some of the heavy coating on a new drumhead. The venerated brush master Ed Thigpen made a practice of doing this on any new drumhead he encountered. This trick guarantees that the drum will not produce a raspy or harsh sound when the brush sweeps across it. It will, instead, sing!

If you don't have any sandpaper, find an appropriate moment to rub back and forth across the head with one of your brushes until some of the coating of that new drumhead comes off. Calfskin or synthetic calf-like heads will not present this problem.

Mallets

Any of the various types of mallets covered with yarn or felt are recommended for use on the tom-toms (good for soft, muted sounds) or for suspended cymbal rolls.

TIP: *A stick bag is recommended for the storage and transportation of your sticks, mallets, and brushes. They come in a variety of sizes, styles, colors, and materials, and can be attached to the side of the floor tom-tom for easy access while playing. Stand-alone stick bags are also available.*

Bass Drum Beaters

Various types of beaters are available for the bass drum pedal. Here are brief descriptions of the most commonly used beaters found on the market.

MEDIUM FELT BEATER: This is a good, general-purpose beater capable of producing a medium punch or fatter attack. It is denser than the large felt beater, and is good for medium-volume music. This is my preferred beater.

LARGE FELT BEATER (sometimes referred to as a lamb's wool beater): This beater is larger than a medium felt beater, and less dense. It is primarily used to produce a tone that is deeper in timbre, but not usually one with a loud punch or attack.

RUBBER BEATER: Because this beater is denser than one made of felt, it will deliver a stronger punch. It will not, however, produce as much punch or attack as one made of plastic or wood.

WOOD/PLASTIC BEATER: Beaters made of plastic or wood are very dense. Wood beaters are generally heavy. They are capable of producing very powerful and sharp attacks, and are especially good for rock and Afro-Cuban applications.

TWO-WAY BEATER: A combination of felt on one side and hard plastic on the other, this beater can produce both tones of felt and wood. Because the plastic side is similar to wood, it is capable of producing a very powerful and sharp attack. Because of its versatility, this beater is used in a variety of musical styles and is offered as a default beater by some pedal manufacturers. Personally, this is not my beater of choice.

PROBLEM: One bass drum, multiple styles.

TIP: *The simplest way to change the sound of a bass drum is to swap out one beater for another. My default beater is a medium-to-hard felt beater.*

In general, we don't like the standard beaters that usually come with pedals. These beaters seem to accentuate attack more than tone (i.e., fundamental low end). I always carry a soft lamb's wool-type beater in my stick bag for those musical occasions where a more gentle, fatter, and/or "cushier" sound is called for. A soft beater will bring out the beauty of your bass drum's low end. For what it's worth, I have found (after 50 years of playing the drums) that a 14" x 20" bass drum is the most versatile one out there.

Pedal Tension Adjustment

Once you've selected the appropriate bass drum beater, adjust
the pedal's spring tension to offer firm resistance to the action of
the foot pedal. The tighter the tension, the faster and stronger the
rebound, but greater effort is required to execute the down stroke.
A looser spring will cause the pedal to be more sluggish and
unresponsive. A medium-spring tension will usually provide the
best of both worlds. I like to adjust my pedal to a degree I call
"sweet resistance"…kind of like Goldilocks and the Three Bears:
not "too…." John J. R. Robinson, on the other hand, prefers a pedal
with tremendous resistance. I'm a lover, not a fighter.

CHOOSING, CHANGING, AND TUNING DRUMHEADS

Drumhead Selection

The majority of today's drumheads are made of plastic or other synthetic materials. Batter heads vary in thickness (thin, medium, and thick, i.e., 2-ply) and may be either transparent or opaque. Though not affected by humidity, plastic heads can be affected by temperature, making them brittle during cold weather. Calfskin heads, which were once used for all drums, remain available but are no longer so common due to price and maintenance factors. When used, they are more appropriate for symphonic use (concert bass drum, timpani, etc.) at the university or professional level.

NOTE: *I love synthetic drumheads, but you really owe it to yourself to play on calfskin heads once in your lifetime. It's the way drumming used to be, and you will marvel at the feel and sound. Every drummer owes it to himself or herself to experience this. It's almost as good as visiting the Grand Canyon.*

Obtaining the Correct Drum Sound

Drumheads come in a variety of types, sizes, finishes, and weights to accommodate the specific needs of drumset players in a variety of musical idioms (country, jazz, rock, pop, R&B, hip-hop, Afro-Cuban, samba, etc.). Each type of drumhead provides a specific sound, texture, and response. The correct drum sound depends on a number of factors the player must be aware of, including the style of music being played and how drum sounds are used in different settings. For example, concert and jazz drumming will generally require a medium-thick head, while marching and rock drumming will typically require a thicker head. In any event, the choice of head and the tuning of the top and bottom heads in relation to each other can have a dramatic impact on the sound you'll get.

When Should a Drumhead Be Replaced?

If the drumhead looks beat, it's probably time to change it. Drumheads should be replaced immediately if torn or broken. They should also be replaced on a regular basis when the heads become worn (certainly if the coating has worn away and you are playing brushes). The quality of sound diminishes over time as the drum is played; therefore, heads that are played loud and long (such as marching or heavy rock applications) will need to be changed more frequently than those played modestly and moderately (such as concert and/or jazz applications).

TIP: *Loosen the head just a bit. If it sags or dents appear, replace it. (Sometimes it's easier to "see" a dead drumhead than to hear it...)*

Materials Needed for Replacing a Drumhead

Essentials
- New head
- Drum key
- Soft cloth

Helpful Materials
- Torque wrench (for marching drums)
- White lithium grease (Vaseline collects too much dust)
- Damp rag and mild soap
- Metal polish
- Furniture polish
- Flat-head or Phillips screwdriver (for removing the wire snares)
- Silicone spray (Uline, 3M, WD-40, etc.)
- Hole-cutting template (optional)
- Muffling materials (tape, gauze, foam, felt strips, pillow, etc.)

Changing a Drumhead

Determine the size of the drum by measuring from one side to the other, shell to shell (outside the drum to determine the drum's diameter) directly across the center. Do not include the hoop when measuring. Or, you can simply match the new head to the old head's size! Obviously, if you know you have a 12" tom, you should get a 12" head for it.

NOTE: *If you're replacing the head on a vintage drum, you should explore Remo's Classic Fit series.*

Select the proper replacement head, and check to make sure it is free from any defects, especially where the head enters the hoop.

Place the head, hoop down, onto a smooth countertop surface to see if it is straight.

Remove the tension rods, counterhoop, and drumhead from your drum.

Clean the counterhoop and wipe the bearing edge of the shell clean. Wood and pearl finishes can be cleaned with a damp cloth and mild soap, and furniture polish may also be applied to wood finishes, if desired. Metal shells and hoops may be cleaned with a damp cloth and/or metal polish.

Before putting the new head in place, a thin coat of paraffin wax may be applied around the bearing edge of the drum shell (this is optional).

NOTE: *This is only necessary on a drum that experiences pitch changes often, such as with timpani. Many timpanists prefer the use of Teflon tape versus paraffin wax.*

Set the new drumhead on the drum shell, and position it so the logo on the drumhead lines up with the air hole, the drum shell logo, or the snare strainer.

Place the counterhoop over the drumhead, and carefully replace the tension rods after lubricating them with white lithium grease or light machine oil. Using your fingers, systematically screw each tension rod in place and tighten them using only slight finger pressure.

Tuning the Various Drums of the Kit

All double-headed drums have a batter and a resonant side or head. Both heads of a single drum do not have to be the same type, and head selection will again be determined by the musical situation, as well as the individual player's taste.

The Cross-Tension System (Recommended)

Before tuning, it will be helpful to number each tension rod by making a mental note, using either the logo or air hole as a point of reference for tension rod #1.

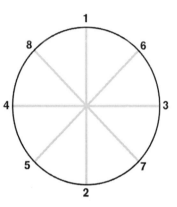

Tune each drum starting with the batter side. When incorporated into a drumset, the snare drum is usually tuned higher than the bass drum and tom-toms. Starting with tension rod #1, use a drum key or torque wrench (for marching drums) to tighten each rod one-half turn (or twist of the wrist). Do this repeatedly until the drumhead feels firm. Be sure not to tension any lug more than you do the others.

Once the initial tensioning of the drumhead is complete, you may get the head in tune with itself by point tuning. Point tuning is achieved by tapping the head with a drumstick about two inches from each rod, to be certain the pitch is consistent all the way around the drum. If it is not, adjust any location where the pitch is lower than average by turning the nearest tension rod clockwise as needed. Adjust any location where the pitch is higher than average by turning the nearest tension rod counterclockwise as needed.

TIP: *For the snare drum, be sure to disengage the snares with the throw-off switch before beginning this step.*

TIP: *It is advisable to muffle the bottom head with something soft (like a pillow) while point tuning the top head, and vice versa. You can set the tom on your drum throne to achieve this same result. This will eliminate the problem of both heads resonating simultaneously, making it easier to point tune each individual head.*

The Clockwise System

As with the cross-tension system, number each tension rod using either the logo or air hole as a point of reference for tension rod #1.

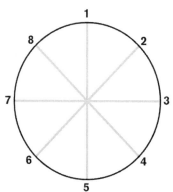

Starting with tension rod #1, tighten each rod one twist of the wrist, moving sequentially around the drum in a circle.

The "tips" mentioned in the cross-tension system section apply to the clockwise system as well.

Setting the Head

1. Once the head is in place and the correct tension has been achieved, take the palm of your hand and place it in the center of the drumhead.

2. Place your other hand on top and press firmly on the head with both hands.

A cracking or popping sound is normal—it is simply the new head adjusting to the tension. Once this is done, the head will hold the tension consistently wherever you set it. Some tough guys like to punch their heads. Careful, as you could hurt your wrist. And, whatever you do, don't ever attempt to punch your hand through a drumhead like that guy in the film *Whiplash*... all you'll do is break your wrist.

3. Make additional adjustments as needed.

THE SNARE DRUM (SPECIFICALLY)

The procedure for tuning the snare head is the same as for the batter head, but with one additional step. Before changing the head, remove the snares on the bottom side of the drum. (It is only necessary to disconnect the snares from one end of the drum.) Once the head has been replaced, reconnect the snares.

Tension the snare head firmly, but be sure that it is still able to vibrate freely against the snares. Some drummers tighten the batter head tighter than the snare, while others do the reverse. There is no firm rule—it is simply a matter of tone preference.

After achieving the desired pitch and tension for both heads, tap the batter head with a drumstick while adjusting the snare adjustment screw until the snares have been brought into contact with the snare head and the desired sound has been achieved.

Be careful not to over-tighten the drumheads or the snares, as you will choke the drum's sound. Remember that sound is produced by allowing the heads and snares to vibrate freely.

Test repeatedly by tapping the head lightly with a drumstick while making adjustments.

QUESTION: How do *you* tune your snare drum?

ANSWER: I usually tune the snare drum at a medium tension on the batter side, and tighter on the bottom head. The snares are tight but not choking the drumhead.

TIP: *If your snare drum has a particularly deep snare bed (this can be spotted by the level of dip in the drum's bearing edge where the snares are positioned and the snare wires or strap connect to the drum), then you may notice a slight amount of wrinkling in the snare head. If this is the case, here's a terrific solution. Get a heat gun, and very carefully apply heat to the head/film at the snare bed on both sides of the drum. This will set the head against the edge of the drum and eliminate any wrinkling.*

To check your snare wire adjustment, tap on the snares with your finger (with the drum in an upside-down position). You should hear "snare" if you're tapping in the middle of the drum (i.e., snare wires), but not near the edge where the snare wires are mounted onto their frame. This tells you if the wires are set properly in the snare bed.

When checking the tuning of the bottom head, disengage the snare strainer (i.e., turn the snares "off"), and place a drumstick between the snappy wires and the drumhead (place the stick flat across the hoop); this way, you can check the pitch of the head without any snare buzzing.

Finally, it bears mentioning that the quality of your drum's sound may rely greatly on the quality of the snare wires. I often turn to third-party snare wire brands for my snare drums.

THE TOM-TOMS (SPECIFICALLY)

There are three possible ways to tune a double-headed drum.

1. Tuning the top and bottom heads to the same pitch will produce a pure tone and a long sustain.

2. Tuning the bottom head lower than the top will produce a deeper sound with a good sustain.

3. Tuning the bottom head tighter than the top will produce a shallower sound with a shorter sustain.

It should be noted that, once you have the top or batter head at a playing tension you're comfortable with, changing the tension of the bottom head can dramatically affect the tone and tuning of any drum. For what it's worth, the Los Angeles studio scene's standard for tuning toms has a protocol or method of tuning the bottom head approximately a minor-third interval higher than the batter head. You heard it here first.

TIP: *Place your tom on a drum throne when setting a new head and making your initial tuning adjustments. The cushiness of the throne material acts as a damper of the inert head.*

QUESTION: How do *you* tune your toms?

ANSWER: I usually tune the bottom head of the toms a major second or minor third higher than the top head. The top head is usually at a medium tension.

MULTIPLE TOMS (SPECIFICALLY)

Multiple tom-toms of varied diameters should be tuned from high to low as one moves from left to right. Some players prefer tuning the three tom-toms of a standard five-piece set using a triad (a three-note chord consisting of a root, third, and fifth) with the bass drum tuned to a fourth below the low tom (also called the *floor tom*). Think of the drums in your drumset as voices in a choir, and simply tune them in a high-to-low relationship.

Multiple toms are indicated in such works as Leonard Bernstein's *Symphonic Dances from West Side Story*. Some drummers will set the four toms up alongside the drumset (either to the left or the right side), with the "high" drum on the right side, much like a keyboard. Me? I like to play the tom part high to low with the smallest tom in the usual two-rack tom position, just in front of the snare drum and over the bass drum. If you've played the drumset for as long as I have, you'll find it easiest to play multiple tom parts this way, even if the written part requires you to come up with some double-stickings or specific hand starts here and there.

THE BASS DRUM (SPECIFICALLY)

Drumset bass drums are referred to as the front head when viewed from the audience and the back head when viewed from the player's perspective.

A solid, front bass drum head that is tuned properly with the batter head can provide a huge, punchy sound. When the heads are tuned up in pitch (such as in a jazz idiom), a very musical, resonant sound can be produced, something that works well with smaller bass drums.

QUESTION: How do you tune your bass drum?

ANSWER: For the small bass drum (18" x 14") I don't use any muffling, except maybe a Muff Bone or a KickPro small pad on the outside of the beater (batter) head. The front (resonant) head is wide open. Lately I've been using the new REMO Felt Tone drumhead. It's just the perfect amount of dampening for that bass drum. For my 20" x 14" drum, I use a REMO Clear Powerstroke 3 for the batter side, and a Fiberskyn 3 or Powerstroke 3 Diplomat for the resonant side (no hole). For my 22" x 14" drum I use the same heads as the 20," but with a 4" or 5" hole in the front head for easy microphone access, and a KickPro pillow (large) inside the drum and against the batter side.

MUFFLING

The desired balance of dampening and resonance may be achieved by selecting the right type of head.

In various musical or studio situations, a certain amount of ring or harmonic overtones may need to be removed from the sound. In order to reduce the desired amount of head resonance, drums can be muffled in a variety of ways, including placing tape, gauze, foam, or other materials on the surface of the drumhead. Remember that placing any material on the head will reduce the resonance and projection of the drum.

QUESTION: How do you muffle your drums?

ANSWER: Most instances of my muffling the toms will occur in the recording studio. While all drumhead manufacturers offer differing versions of plastic "rings" (one-inch-wide rings that fit each drum size based on its circumference), I prefer to use a cloth version of this idea, known as EQ Roots. You can also use gel squares or dots designed for this purpose.

Several companies manufacture effective muffling systems that will provide adequate and adjustable muffling. Remo's new Felt Tone head has a built-in muffle strip. This works great as a resonant head and prevents you from having to place a felt strip between the shell and the head.

The Snare Drum

If more dampening is desired, additional muffling can be achieved by placing a small amount of duct tape or a piece of cloth to the top exterior of the batter head, near the edge.

TIP: *If nothing else, using your wallet will work in a jam. We suggest hanging half of it on the drumhead, with the other half hanging off the rim of the drum. I prefer the Drum Wallet versus my own wallet, as I might leave it on the drum and not be able to pay for lunch!*

Using the internal muffler included with some models is not recommended; it muffles the head by applying pressure from the head's underside, restricting the natural resonance of the drum. After a certain amount of use, it may also create a rattling noise.

The Bass Drum

Felt strips may be placed behind both heads of the bass drum. Some players may choose to place a pillow, blanket, or piece of foam rubber inside the drum. In this case, the cost is minimal, and the sound can be customized to fit your needs.

Portable/external bass drum mufflers are very useful, whether you use a clamp-on device such as the Gary Chaffee Bass Drum Muffler, or the Paul Kreibich PK's Original Muffbone. If nothing else, a small towel or a folded-up newspaper stuffed between the bass drum pedal yoke (frame), and the bass drum head can dampen just enough ring to make your bass drum more stylistically appropriate. Synthetic dots work well sonically but, in our experience, tend to fall off the vertical surface of the bass drum head.

A bass drum should not be too "dead" or over muffled. Any and every drum needs tone and some ring in order for it to project its sound.

Front bass drum heads may also be purchased either with a six-inch hole cut off-center, or with a larger center hole. (If you would like to cut your own hole, the use of a hole-cutting template will allow you to choose your own placement.) The front hole allows air to escape, resulting in a more direct sound while retaining some of the resonant qualities of the front head. It also allows a microphone to be placed inside the drum at varying degrees.

TIP: *Most drum companies provide their hole in the head at an approximate position of 5 o'clock. Engineers hate this, as it makes access to the hole difficult. A 3 o'clock position works better, as it allows the engineer to easily place a mic inside the bass drum. If you've ever wondered why some drummers have their front bass drum heads at an odd angle with the drum name/logo crooked, that's why.*

PERFORMANCE AND RECORDING TIPS

Attitude

Drummers are the bus drivers of the band. The airline pilot for the players. The generalissimo leading the jazzers. The Rocker of Gibraltar. The lion tamer walking into that cage, and so on.

When you walk into any playing situation, one with friends or with complete strangers, project quiet confidence and command, because *that's* the gig. We're in charge of making the music feel as good as possible and keeping the tempo honest. We're also responsible for the overall dynamic level of any ensemble we play in.

NOTE: *If you need to play softly, consider and watch what parts of the kit you're striking, as some parts will generate a lot more waveforms and excite more frequencies than others. By "excite" we mean using up more frequency space, thus obliterating other parts of the group/music. It's all in the orchestration, as well as in the touch.*

In terms of how *much* to play, I get a lot of my inspiration from Clint Eastwood, as his characters always seem to become quieter before they take bigger actions. I once got the opportunity to talk to Clint about this, and he said, "Yeah…I hold it in and then let it out, a little at a time…"

As the drummer, you need to take *ownership* of:

- the beat
- the idea
- a compositional turn

When Steve Gadd plays, he shows ownership, which is part of what makes his unique drumming style so cool.

Mel Lewis…*attitude*…which he possessed even as a young drummer. And *that* may just be a gift from the gods.

Too much calling attention to oneself, however, is *not* a good thing. Elvin Jones and Tony Williams somehow knew how to balance the hip drum stuff with the forward momentum of the tune, whether "live" or in the studio.

You will create more intensity that way.

Bus driver. Pilot. Lion tamer. Clint Eastwood. Steve Gadd. Elvin.

Get it?

What Do Other Musicians Say?

Below are some quotes from my very first drum book, *Drum Concepts and Techniques*, written when I was all of 30 years old. I asked several colleagues for their best advice to drummers, and got the following responses:

"You play the drums, I'll play the guitar." *–John Scofield*

"Don't play so loud." *–Randy Brecker*

"And, don't play a fill every two bars." *–Eliane Elias*

"Make me sound good." *–John Abercrombie*

"Never pet a burning dog." *–Steve Gadd*

"Play that wide, fat beat that I can drive a Mack Truck through. I like that." *–Marc Johnson*

And this timeless quote from Papa Jo Jones: "Always start basic and you'll never go wrong...after you have control of your instrument, you can do whatever you wish. Regardless of whatever they name it: *you play.*"

Some of *my* advice from that book includes:

- Show up early for every gig, and be ready to go!
- Play what the music requires.
- Set up so you can have eye contact with the other musicians.
- Keep your instrument in good working condition.
- Stay healthy.
- Warm up.

QUESTION: How soon should I be set up and ready to play before the downbeat?

ANSWER: At least 15 minutes. As the saying goes, "If you're early you're on time, if you're on time you're late, and if you're late you're fired!" Give yourself plenty of time to get to the gig in case something goes wrong (a flat tire, wrong directions, an accident on the freeway, a lane closure, etc.), so you can be set up and ready to play between 15 to 30 minutes before the downbeat. Being early and relaxed lets the client and/or bandleader know you're a pro, and helps contribute to the overall success of the gig. If it's a recording session, the norm is for everyone to be in the studio ready to go one hour before the downbeat, and that means the drums are set up and ready to be mic'ed at least one hour before the session is scheduled to begin.

QUESTION: Should I bring an additional snare drum and cymbals to work?

ANSWER: In most cases, this should not be necessary. Your drums are your drums, your instrument is your instrument, and you are *you*. But, there may be occasions when having alternate snare and cymbal options will give you a competitive edge. For recording work, I will usually bring an extra cymbal bag with various ride, crash, and splash cymbals, so I'm covered for any style or genre (particularly when "period" music is being played). The same holds true for snare drums. A bright snare with a fair amount of ring, tuned high with plenty of overtones, might be perfect for jazz, whereas a darker, lower-tuned snare (possibly of deeper depth) will be better suited for a funk, fusion, or rhythm-and-blues track. How much gear you want to carry around is up to you.

My professor used to ask, "What are you doing this weekend?" And I would reply, "I'm playing this gig or that." He would then challenge me to "only take a bass drum, snare drum, and hi-hat to the gig," to which I would reply, "No, I need to have all of my drums for this gig." Why? Well, I'm sure that my reasons were musically valid, but it also had to do with the fact I wanted to be able to impress anyone who might be listening by having my full arsenal of drums and cymbals handy. *His* point was that by reducing the number of playing surface options, I would have to be more creative in my drumming. If I could go back in time, I would follow his suggestion. In fact, since that time, I will often challenge myself in this way. The results are always surprisingly creative and hip! Just saying.

QUESTION: What accessory percussion instruments are indispensable?

ANSWER: For live and/or recording work a cowbell (I prefer a low-pitched bell with an optional mount), a woodblock (mounted), tambourines (both free-standing and mounted…mounted tambourines are almost always headless), a shaker (for soft playing, you can choose an egg-shaped shaker—plastic or metal tube shakers will give you more dynamic range), a triangle & beater, wind chimes (also known as bar chimes, bell trees, or Mark trees), and a cabasa (normally played by hand, though I prefer the pedal-operated version manufactured by Meinl).

My instrument collection contains multiple cowbells, woodblocks, shakers, and tambourines. Some of these vary by pitch, and some by material (brass jingles vs. copper vs. aluminum for the tambourines; plastic or metal tubes for shakers, with varying sizes and weights of shot—those invisible sandy-sounding things that produce the shaker sound), etc. You may mount your cowbell and/or woodblock on the bass drum hoop by means of a clamp, or from a cymbal stand by means of an accessory mount designed for that purpose.

Other mountable percussion accessories include the Brazilian tamborim and pandeiro (Meinl sells a combination of these two percussion instruments, called a "Tampeiro"), agogo bells, guiro, cabasa, steel plates, etc. Most of these are played with sticks, brushes, or mallets, but the cabasa is best played by hand.

Other pedal-controlled percussion instruments include the cowbell, woodblock, tambourine, and cajón.

Some drummers like to produce exotic sounds by placing small cymbals on top of their snare or tom batters, or small percussive objects on top of their cymbals. Most of these drummers live in New York City.

QUESTION: Do drummers need to know music theory, too?

ANSWER: While there are some famous drummers who can't read music, they are the exception and not the rule. The very best drummers are those who have some background in music theory. Studying a melodic instrument, such as a piano or mallets, will give you a valuable understanding of harmony, chord structure, etc. You need to know about song forms before you can navigate through a chart, or even play a tune without reading a chart. You must be able to visualize the form in your head. Hearing and recognizing harmonic function helps!

Quick! You're playing Duke Ellington's "Take the A Train," and the band stops at the bridge of the tune for you to play a short break or solo. How many bars do you play? (You can find the answer on the next page.)

ANSWER to "A Train" question: Eight bars.

Knowing harmony makes it easier to recognize and play melodies at the drums. You know those big spaces between some notes of a drum solo? Learn to trust the music enough to give those long notes the intentional weight (not *loud*, but the weight of *intent*) to "sell" them to the listener…and

in this case

the ultimate listener is *you.*

Don't worry about always trying to make your drumming interesting. Just focus on making it real.

PROBLEM: I'm playing conscientiously with good dynamics, but my drums sound *too loud* in the audience. What am I doing wrong?

SOLUTION: Try to avoid snare hits that combine the rim with the drumhead! Drummers do this *far more often* than they realize, and while this can be a terrific way to get a cracking backbeat sound on the snare drum, it is overused to poor effect when playing accents. This combined sound of the rim plus the head takes up more sonic space than you might expect, and in a "live" room or hall, the resulting sound is deadly to the music. It sounds like noise, so stop it.

PROBLEM: How do I keep my drums from sliding while playing?

TIP: *There are a number of commercially available products such as a bass drum anchor that attaches to the bottom of the front counterhoop (more of a vintage drum item), or non-slip drum mats/rugs. In a pinch, you can do what drummers did in the old days, and simply attach one end of a rope to your bass drum, and the other end to your throne.*

PROBLEM: I'm experiencing too much ringing in my ears.

TIP: *Exposure to playing drums and listening to loud amplified music without ear protection can create a temporary or permanent ringing in the ears, called "tinnitus." Ear protection is the only way to prevent noise-induced hearing loss. Earplugs are small inserts that fit snuggly into the outer ear canal. They are available for purchase in a variety of shapes and sizes, or they can be custom made. We suggest you always carry a pair for protection during sound check or to provide silent relief in noisy public places. Do not insert ordinary cotton balls or tissue paper wads into the ear canal, as they are very poor protectors.*

NOTE: *Hearing damage is not reversible.*

PROBLEM: Because I have sweaty hands, how can I avoid dropping a stick while playing?

TIP: *There are a number of commercially available products on the market such as grip tape, stick wax, drumming gloves, sticks dipped in a rubber-like coating, etc. Some drummers use antiperspirant lotion on their hands, sand their sticks in the grip area for greater friction, or purchase sticks that are not lacquered. Experiment to see which of these solutions work best for you.*

Mics and Drums

I generally leave mic choices and placement up to the engineer, whether on stage or in the studio. Depending on the style or sound of the music, I may make a suggestion regarding a specific mic for a particular drum, such as the bass drum. If I'm playing an 18" bass drum tuned up in pitch, I may not want a bass drum mic that brings out or "bumps" the low end. I will also take note of the placement of a bass drum mic to the resonant head. If it's too close, that may produce what is known as the "proximity effect," which results in an unnatural and exaggerated low end to the sound (otherwise known as a "whoof").

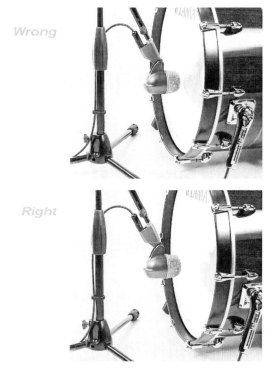

Condenser mics are great but are more prone to feedback on stage than dynamic mics.

QUESTION: The engineer is getting too much "ring" from my snare drum and is asking me to dampen it. What should I do?

ANSWER: Suggest altering the mic's placement. In general, if a mic is placed too close to the edge of a drum versus pointed more towards the center, it will "hear" too much ring. Sometimes moving a mic's position in relation to the drum will achieve the desired sound rather than you having to re-tune or dampen your drums, etc.

However your drums sound at home, they will undoubtedly sound different in a studio. The same goes for a concert hall or club. The room is the *nth* member of the band!

You'll also want to make sure the engineer pays attention to the careful placement of the overhead mics. The two overhead mics should be evenly distanced from the snare drum—otherwise the snare drum will be out of phase.

Most engineers know all of these things. Whenever I'm working with an engineer for the first time, I will shake his or her hand while introducing myself, and ask the engineer to let me know if any of my drums are "misbehaving" in the room, etc. This lets him or her know that it's okay to make tuning suggestions, and creates a sense of trust in the workplace. Both of us may now proceed to work towards getting the best sound as partners rather than a case of musician-against-engineer. Remember, everyone is trying to do the best job possible.

ADVICE: *Be nice to your engineers...they control and determine your mix.*

PROBLEM: I can't hear the actual volume of my drums when I'm wearing headphones.

TRICK: Pull the right or left headset off your ear, so that one ear is receiving the audio information from the headset, while the other ear is hearing the sound of your drums in the room. Keeping the "pulled" headset side flush against your head will prevent any audio leakage from bleeding into your drum mics.

This is a trick or technique I employ often in the studio, sometimes for just a few seconds so I can reassure myself of the "actual" or "pre-mic" sound my drums are making in the studio environment. Again, the drums' sound can be charged drastically by the reverberant qualities of a room, and the one-ear-on/one-ear-off trick always lets me know what the instrument and touch truly sound like before they're mic'ed, processed, and mixed.

TIP: *It's always a good idea to invite the engineer out to the drums and play them so he or she can hear what the drums sound like from your location. This provides a reference point for expectations. I do this onstage with front-of-house engineers as well. It's important to know what a drumset sounds like without the microphones (or, "without all of the assistance," as Buddy Rich once put it).*

NOTE: *If you're in the studio and wearing headphones while the engineer is getting sounds or adjusting knobs, etc., you might want to get into the habit of keeping the phones half-on/half-off your ears, so if there IS a malfunction where a loud noise is sent out to the headphones, you'll minimize the potential damage to your hearing. We speak from experience on this.*

PROBLEM: I'm recording, and this recording will last forever.

SOLUTION: Relax. It's merely a snapshot. Hopefully your eyes aren't closed when the picture is taken. It's merely a moment in time. Just concentrate and have fun.

QUESTION: Do you have any particular mic preferences when it comes to your drums?

ANSWER: I generally use Shure mics, and always trust their SM7 or Beta 52 for the bass drum. However, I can also recommend the Sennheiser 421 for 18" jazz- or bebop-tuned bass drums (or the Audio-Technica AE2500 Dual Element mic), or the good ol' AKG D112. For toms, I love the Shure Beta clip-on mics, and you can't beat an SM57 for the snare. Overheads? Check out their Beta 181 mics.

TRICKS OF THE TRADE

The following section includes random tips and tricks, delivered in bite-sized bits of information, which will address a number of drumming issues and solutions. The topics in this section are random, and are presented in no particular order.

QUESTION: Should I twirl my sticks?

ANSWER: No.

QUESTION: What other stick tricks are available?

ANSWER: Plenty.

Dead sticking into your drums and cymbals can produce a really cool sound. When using light pressure, this technique can be employed in the middle of drum fills (Mel Lewis often did this simultaneously on the floor tom and the snare). It's a very cool way to widen the beat, but don't *overdo* this when comping.

TIP: *Playing rim clicks on two drums at once!*

TRICK: Instead of playing a cross-stick on the snare rim alone, try playing it on the adjacent rack tom, and bring the stick down onto the snare rim in the same motion (I first heard this flam effect used by a Brazilian drummer).

TIP: *Play the ride cymbal with a stick and the snare drum with a brush!* This *sounds so cool.*

PROBLEM: A triplet played on the hi-hat by any other name is a *what*?

TRICK: Let's call it a hat-let. Check this out.

If you're familiar with the triplet being played on the drumset as follows (Right – Left – Kick, Right – Left – Kick, Right – Left – Kick, Right – Left – Kick), then you might know that the sticking for this lick can also be played (Right – Left – Kick, Left – Right – Kick, etc.). In other words, the foot stays in the same place, but the hands alternate their place within the tuplet.

R L K R L K R L K R L K R L K R L K R L K R L K

R L K L R K R L K L R K R L K L R K R L K L R K

While this lick is most-often played utilizing the bass drum, here's a really cool way to incorporate the hi-hat into this mix.

- Start by playing the hi-hat using only the foot or pedal.
- Begin with the following sticking, playing Right – Left on the snare drum or any combination of two drums on the kit:
  Right – Left – Hat Pedal, Right – Left – Hat Pedal,
  Right – Left – Hat Pedal, etc.

R L H R L H R L H R L H R L H R L H R L H R L H

• Go back and try this sticking: Right – Left – Hat Pedal,
Left – Right – Hat Pedal, Right – Left – Hat Pedal,
Left – Right – Hat Pedal, etc.

R L H L R H R L H L R H   R L H L R H R L H L R H

Now, move the right hand onto the closed hi-hat, and play the snare drum with the left hand.

R L H R L H R L H R L H   L R H L R H L R H L R H

Do the "Elvin Jones," alternating hands as follows between the snare and hi-hat surfaces, still activating the hi-hat pedal on every third tuplet of each triplet: Right – Left – Hat Pedal, Left – Right – Hat Pedal, Right – Left – Hat Pedal, Left – Right – Hat Pedal, etc.

R L H L R H R L H L R H   R L H L R H R L H L R H

Wow! Do you hear what's happening? The hi-hat is enjoying the open/closing action of the foot, which is merely trying to play the hi-hat on the third tuplet. However, the hands (the right hand, specifically) are catching the hi-hat in an "open" state, when it's just about to close, every other time.

The result is one of the slickest moves in jazz drumming. Start slowly and gradually build up the speed. And, remember to be conscious of balance. It's the balance that sells most any drumset idea.

Enjoy your hatlets, and you're welcome.

"Be still my beating heart (and my bouncing leg)."

PROBLEM: My hi-hat leg bounces too much for no good reason.

TIP: *Stop it.*

BACKGROUND: When I was a member of the group Weather Report, founder, keyboardist, and leader Joe Zawinul once asked me to play a beat for him. When I did he noticed that my left leg was bouncing up and down in rhythm even though it was not being used to play the (hi-hat) pedal. "What's going on with your leg?" he asked. "What do you mean? I'm just moving it in time..." "No," he interrupted, "Put that energy into what you are playing."

This is insanely good advice. It not only serves to focus your musical energy to where it needs to be going, it also ensures that you are internalizing the beat versus externalizing the beat. The time is not in our elbows or forearms, or thighs or legs...the time is in our minds and hearts, and the more relaxed our limbs are, the more quickly and smoothly we can respond to any and every whim of our creative imaginations.

Try playing all of this with the *heel down* on the hi-hat. The motor and bounce distraction is making itself felt and heard in small but noticeable ways.

This ties in with...

PROBLEM: There's too much movement—the sticks are up in the air and out of position. This is an invitation for musical "gremlins" to creep into your playing.

TIP: *Keep your sticks where they're working.*

OPINION: Playing the drums should feel like a friendly game of cards, *not* like guiding a Boeing 787 into its parking spot on the airport tarmac. Just like any physical activity, efficiency in movement is the key to success. Check out the great drummers (as in the great jazz drummers). There's not a whole lot of sticks-up-in-the-air business going on. Why? Because they knew better. Sticks in the air are for show; sticks near your drumheads and cymbals are for music.

CONTINUED: *Play with less vertical motion, and think of more horizontal movement around the drums. Keep all strokes simple. The less extraneous the motion, the better. Stay low to the instrument.*

PROBLEM: What's the best way to move around a drumset?

TIP: *Pivot, and posture.*

Pay attention to how you sit at the drums. Are you sitting on your legs (thighs), or are you sitting on your "rockers" or "sit bones"?

Rotate your pelvis so your imaginary tail sticks out at a 45-degree angle behind you. Your chest should be open to the world (and the music), with your shoulders pulled back and not hunched forward. Your body, mind, and soul will be more receptive to musical input, and your back will feel much better after any rehearsal, practice session, or gig.

Now that you're seated properly (with your knees slightly lower than your hips, and with your feet slightly in front of your knees), you can concentrate and focus on moving your sticks around the kit. You're in the drumming cockpit now. You shouldn't have to reach too far in order to strike any part of the kit, nor rotate or twist your torso in the extreme as well. Want to play that floor tom? Pivot your wrist in order to strike it quickly and effectively. Buddy Rich did this when he played his floor tom. It saves time, motion, and energy.

Relax your shoulders. You're not going to swing if your body is tense.

This advice extends to your mouth as well. A tight jaw and pursed lips equal a tight beat. Look at photos of such drummers as Art Blakey (mouth open, tongue hanging out); Tony Williams (mouth open much of the time); Elvin Jones (same). Papa Jo Jones (okay… smiling). Relax, and enjoy! This is supposed to be fun.

PLUS: *Don't forget to breathe when you play. Breathing not only makes all things possible, it will also help you to relax, and will have a most positive effect on your musical phrasing.*

PROBLEM: You're giving me a lot of good advice, but it's too much to think about when I'm playing!

TIP: *Don't think. Concentrate!*

OPINION: "Practice is for the practice room. When you're in front of an audience, forget mechanics…relax, concentrate, and create."
−Bill Platt, principal percussionist of the Cincinnati Symphony Orchestra (40 years, now retired)

QUESTION: How high should I position my music stand?

ANSWER: If you position your music stand to the left of the kit, then no higher than your hi-hat cymbals. Placing the stand higher than this, especially when working with other musicians, puts a wall between you and the rest of the band. Eye contact and visual communication are vitally important in any ensemble.

The same advice holds true for when you position the stand in front of you or to the right side of the kit. If you need to make page turns, then having the music stand in front of the kit makes that job nearly impossible. When working with an orchestra or during similar situations where you need to follow a conductor, scan the music to be played, convert those scans to PDF files, and use an iPad with a remote page-turning device (made operable by Bluetooth technology) that can be controlled by your left hand or one of your feet.

I prefer to control page turns by using my left hand on the pedal switcher. I keep the iPad's height as low as possible so as to maintain optimal eye contact, and to preserve the best-possible sightline for the audience.

CHALLENGE: Counting while reading

TIP: *While I do not count while I am playing something notated on a page of music, I do count when I need to keep track of rests and how many bar numbers will pass before I make my next entrance. It's easy to lose track of the count—examples include film sessions where the music or onscreen action distracts you, or hearing one thing but seeing "another" in terms of the bar or the layout of the measures, etc. So, I use my fingers and count intently, with intention! It's okay to use your fingers to count. I'm a grown man, and I do it all of the time—discreetly, of course. I start with my thumb and then add each finger one measure at a time, touching the thumb with that finger until I reach "five," and then starting all over again ("six...seven..." and so on). The tactile connection seems to help me keep score.*

If you're working with a click track, that makes it relatively easy to know where the beat is; otherwise, be sure to keep an eye on the conductor while you're reading and/or counting!

PROBLEM: Talk, talk, talk, talk.

TIP: *The less said, the better.*

BACKGROUND: Many years ago, when I was first starting out in the New York City studio scene, I found myself in a studio recording music for a new television program. The producer of the program was fairly well known, and the composer/producer of the session was a gentleman I had worked with briefly/previously in Los Angeles. I'm not sure why, but I was "feeling my oats" during this evening session—I was rambunctious, loud-mouthed and, looking back, acting like a jerk. The session seemed to go well, musically. Imagine my shock the following morning when I received a telephone call from the composer, who rang me simply to tell me that my "bullsh*t jazz attitude and big mouth were a complete drag, and not at all appreciated by anyone in the control room." Click. I played well enough, but I lost the account because I had to be Mr. Entertainment with my big mouth, negating all of the good work I had done up to that point with this client and others in the studio. As embarrassing and shameful as the phone call was, this guy did me a great favor by waking me up to my own baloney, and teaching me a big lesson.

When working on a project that's not your own (i.e., most of the time for us freelancers), the people in charge have many things on their plate, and the *last* thing anyone needs to worry about is a loud-mouthed drummer. Keep your head low, and do good work.

This also applies to asking questions during a rehearsal or recording session. Certainly ask if there's something you need to know in order to do your best work. Much of the time you should be able to figure out the answer yourself without delaying a project or embarrassing a conductor/composer by asking obvious error questions (i.e., pointing out an error on the written part). You can seek guidance regarding a rhythm or note by asking the lead trumpet player (or another rhythm section player). A little discretion can go a long way in the studio or rehearsal stage. No side talking or joking around. And, for Pete's sake, keep your smartphone away until break time!

READING RHYTHMS

The ability to read music is essential to being a complete musician. There is no reason for anyone to practice or promote illiteracy in any language, music included.

Basic note values and their relative lengths (duration) are simple math. And, just like math, the numbers do not lie. Whatever the time signature, the notes must (and will) add up correctly.

It is *not* necessary to learn how to read really complicated rhythms (with superimposed metric schemes, etc.), although it can't hurt, I guess…but, in all the years I've worked in the studio or with orchestras, big bands, and combos of every description, most of the time I've only had to deal with eighth notes, quarter notes, plus some sixteenths and triplets here and there. Quintuplets or groupings of seven over nine, etc.? Only once in a bad dream about Frank Zappa's music.

That said, I pride myself on being able to read basic note values quickly and reliably in just about any combination. How did I learn to do this? I practiced reading every day, and worked towards speed reading of basic note values, etc.

TIP: *Sing as you play. I enjoy improvising or "composing" an imaginary big band chart (à la Thad Jones) using the written notes for the rhythms. This makes sight-reading a page of snare drum notes an immediately rewarding and interesting musical experience.*

TRICK: If and when you encounter a measure of music with a gobbledygook of rests in the middle, scan forward to the *end* of the measure and read *backwards* (all while you're reading *forward*). I know…it sounds complicated…but it's not. You can very quickly determine that the next note you'll need to play is, for example, on the "+" of beat 3, and you won't have to guess what all of those rests add up to. I refer to this as check-sum reading.

TIP: *Get yourself a copy of the Louie Bellson/Gil Breines book* Modern Reading Text in $\frac{4}{4}$ for All Instruments, *and spend ten minutes a day reading it. You will become a better reader before you know it.*

CHALLENGE: How do you rescue a jazz ballad that's become too slow as a result of the double-time solo section settling too much (check it out... it almost *always* happens).

SOLUTION: At the point of transition, use mallets on a suspended cymbal to create a swell (a distraction!) that functions as a medley ("medley" as in a Broadway overture, etc.) device, allowing the proper tempo to be reinstated without awkwardness. This will save many a tune that have gone too deep into the tempo rabbit hole!

SLOW BALLAD TEMPO TRICK: Incorporate a *silent* double-time heel movement (eighth notes) on the hi-hat pedalboard, while playing a relaxed quarter-note pulse on the snare drum (triplet feel). If you master this, the tempo will *never* slow down while you're playing the drums on a ballad. Tempo is sacred!

CHALLENGE (Over-the-Bar Phrasing): Okay, so you're reading a piece of music and you come across the following metric scheme: One bar of ¾, followed by a bar of ⅜, then a 2/4 measure, followed by another bar of ¾, then ⅜, and, finally, good ol' 4/4. What do you do?

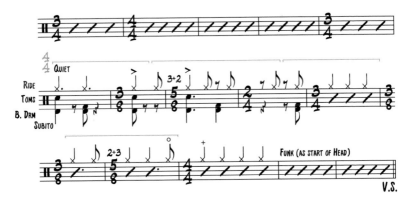

V.S.

ANSWER: There's no shame in graphing a metric scheme above the notated bars of music and using the accent scheme to help determine the strong (or "hip") parts of the overall beat or feel. In the example above, the seven bars of changing meters convert nicely into three bars of 4/4 time! The music can be played in a "drum-istic" way that feels good rather than forced.

When I pointed out this unnecessary challenge (yet pleasant anomaly) to composer Mark-Anthony Turnage, he merely replied, "Oh, yeah. Sorry." This solution reminds me of how my father used to drive his car on windy roads. Traffic allowing, he would "straighten out the road," doing less curves and more straight driving as conditions allowed. Not a bad idea to figure out the horizon line of any piece of music. It will not only feel better, but make you less crazy in the end.

QUESTION: How fast should I play a tremolo (roll) on a suspended (crash or ride) cymbal?

ANSWER: An important factor to keep in mind when playing a roll is that the surface (or membrane) of a cymbal (or tom) is only free to vibrate until it is played again after its initial strike. That is, a cymbal's sustain can be added to, but the initial waveform creation is interrupted each time we play it. The more rapidly we strike the surface, the more percussive the sound becomes. So, you're working against the potential of the instrument to sustain with each successive stroke. The more space between hits, the more the instrument will breathe and sound.

Experiment with this, and you'll find a happy medium for creating sustained rolls. I tend to stick to single strokes when using sticks, and I listen for the colors I'm creating. I might play these strokes on various parts of the cymbal. Mallet rolls are almost always played near the edge for maximum tone. Your cymbals should be allowed to ring freely on their stands.

When playing a crescendo, the intensity of each stroke should build until the desired peak or climax is reached. While it is intuitive to reach a cymbal roll's climax when the rest of the ensemble plays its loud or strong note, I find it effective to time my roll to climax either before or after the ensemble's peak. This overlap creates a most-pleasing effect.

QUESTION: For those occasions when I have to do more than one thing at a time, how can I produce a one-handed suspended cymbal roll?

ANSWER: Using medium-soft mallets made of felt or yarn, hold the two mallets in the same hand (one mallet on top of the cymbal and the other underneath), and move the wrist in an up-and-down motion to produce the roll (*see photos below*). Remember, only roll fast enough to sustain the sound. Whether written into the music, or thought-up on your own, the one-handed mallet roll produces a lovely transition moment in the music.

WHAT ABOUT A DRUM?

If you play too rapidly on a drumhead surface, the vibrations of the head in motion will begin canceling the sound out. Your sound becomes smaller, and the "meaning" of your well-intentioned velocity will get lost in the less-than-optimal sound. If you exceed this speed limit, you begin working against yourself and your best interests. You need to find that tipping point.

CHALLENGE: How do I get the best sound from my sticks, and what should I do when I break one?

TIP *(literally)*: *Inspect the tips of your sticks each time before you begin to play. If a tip is chipped or otherwise damaged, set that stick aside. I'll usually set the tip end of the stick on the floor, and step on the shoulder of the stick in order to break it so I won't use it again. It's not fun to play an entire tune in concert or on a recording session and realize that your dull cymbal sound is because the tip of your ride stick is shot.*

If I break a stick in a performance or studio situation, I drop it onto the carpeted floor, and pick up another stick from my stick bag. *I do not throw the stick up in the air or towards the audience.* Seriously, you could hurt someone that way!

And, before playing a tune or groove that involves a cross-stick, I find the sweet spot of the stick's butt end by placing it on the rim and performing a quick sound check. I will take note of the stick's sweet spot on the rim by eying its location (i.e., seeing where the stick-maker's logo is in relation to the rim).

The result? I always get a great-sounding cross-stick on the snare drum. Always! How? By paying attention. The angels and devils of drumming are in the details.

TIP: *If you want to quickly pick up a stick from your stick bag, we suggest you not keep your sticks encased in the cardboard wrapper they come in, as you'll most likely end up pulling two sticks from your stick bag rather than just one. It's easy for a stick bag to become overloaded and cluttered, so we suggest you periodically do some spring cleaning of your contents. You don't need to carry a lifetime's worth of sticks, mallets, and brushes everywhere you go, and every time you play.*

QUESTION: How can I create a sizzle cymbal without purchasing one, or drilling holes in my existing cymbals?

ANSWER: An emergency or temporary sizzle solution can be achieved by draping a lightweight chain (found in a hardware store's plumbing department) from the top of any cymbal.

CHALLENGE: How can I improve my snare drum roll?

TIP: *For this answer, I turn to the best hands guy I know, Bill Platt.*

"In my opinion, most drummers roll too fast, with too many bounces in each hand and too much downward pressure (i.e., "press roll"). Two notes in each hand is too "open," and four or more notes in each hand is too "pressy." Try three notes in each hand alone, bounced at full speed (i.e., half a roll). Then, put the halves together, alternating hand to hand. This roll is good for mf and louder. For softer dynamics, add additional bounces in each hand, and go for a touch bounce rather than a press.

CHALLENGE: Along those lines, what's the easiest and most reliable way to play a four-stroke ruff?

TIP: *Assuming you can already play double strokes (i.e., bounces) in each hand, try bouncing double strokes in both hands simultaneously. Many times you will not play them exactly together, as one hand will begin slightly ahead of the other. If you're lucky and both hands bounce perfectly together, begin with one hand slightly higher than the other so the hands are slightly "off." You now have the beginning of a hand-to-hand (RLRL or LRLR) four-stroke ruff! Alternate stickings, especially for soft dynamics, include LRRL, RLLR, LLRR, and RRLL.*

CHALLENGE: I am not from Brazil, so how do I play samba?

TIP: *In addition to listening to samba, bossa nova,* or any *style of music you might want to play, there are secrets to phrasing, as well as rhythmic interpretation that will make your drumming life easier. For samba, a couple of things to remember:*

Think of samba in 2, not 4. With the bass drum playing on beats 1 and 2 (without the pick-up note, or "heartbeat" motor, for now), accent on beat 2.

Play eighth notes on the hi-hat (remember: we're in cut time now) using the following sticking: R-L-L-R, R-L-L-R, R-L-L-R, R-L-L-R, etc.

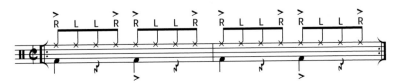

The notes played with the RH should be phrased more like a shuffle, rather than a straight up-and-down subdivision, and the LH notes *should* be played straight up and down (no syncopation or swing). When you combine the two hands in this way, you will enjoy a true samba feel. Here it is, notated in 𝄴/4 time for simplicity's sake:

Here is another terrific way to play an up-tempo samba at a very soft
dynamic, perfect for song intros or working with a vocalist. I also
play a simple bossa-nova rhythm on the hi-hat (using two hands) for
the purpose of playing softly without effort or musical discomfort.
We're back in cut time…all of these examples should be played at the
same hi-hat or subdivision tempo. Don't start too fast, for starters!

Speaking of vocalists…

QUESTION: What is the correct tempo when working with a singer?

ANSWER: Any tempo the singer wants!

Seriously! Vocalists must not only pay attention to pronunciation, but hitting the notes as well—so if the tempo is wrong, no one is happy. Remember, job #1 is being able to provide rhythmic information to the band. Job #1 ½ is being able to find and maintain the correct tempo (which may change from night to night, etc.). Keep your eyes and ears open, as it's better to adjust the tempo to the singer's preference rather than fight and/or allow them to struggle through the delivery of the entire song. Remember, they're telling a story up there. And whether that story ends happily ever after or not could depend on you. A metronome will come in handy to note the "correct" tempo for a song, but this is always subject to change. Keep your eyes and ears open!

Here are some of the vocalists I've worked with: Joni Mitchell, Mary Chapin Carpenter, Linda Ronstadt, Barbra Streisand, Diana Krall, Elvis Costello, Frank Sinatra, Jr., Diane Schuur, Joe Williams, June Christy, The Three Degrees, Melba Moore, Freda Payne, Patti Austin, Tierney Sutton, Steely Dan, Boz Scaggs, Al Jarreau, Michael Feinstein, Michael Bolton, Michael Bublé, Rod Stewart, Natalie Cole, Lizz Wright, Stevie Wonder, Catherine Russell, Stevie Nicks, Sheryl Crow, Katharine McPhee, Seth MacFarlane, Randy Crawford, Pino Daniele, Andrea Bocelli, Roberta Gambarini, Martina McBride, Thomas Quasthoff, plus productions at the Royal Opera House and New York City Opera.

QUESTION: How do I play with a click?

ANSWER: The best way to play to a click track (or metronome) is, of course, to play right with it. But the best *trick* is to "chase" the click instead of allowing yourself to somehow get ahead of it. Experienced studio musicians will most often opt to chase the click track. If you practice with a metronome, we do not recommend you set the click sound on beats 2 and 4, as this is never done in the studio. Learn to swing or play any feel with the metronome sounding on the beat. The more you do it, the more natural the process will become.

TIP: *If I could have done anything differently in my drumming life, I would have practiced much more with a metronome when I was younger. I also would have purchased a copy of* Stick Control, *but that's another story.*

TIMELESS ESTHETICS

Is it just the fact that we were young when we discovered and listened so much to Elvin, Mel, Tony, etc., or is there a timeless strength to their music making (like Picasso and art)? How do we approach this mountain of magnificence in order to attempt to climb it and plant our own flag?

QUESTION: How do I play more "modern"?

ANSWER: More modern doesn't equate to playing busier or louder! Whatever you do, you don't want your drumming to tire the listener or other musicians out. Be creative without being overbearing, conversant without shouting, etc. *Think texture.*

Modern doesn't necessarily mean busier. Its meaning is closer to that of stretching the fabric of the time by *committing* to thematic ideas and rhythmic motivic development…evocation by provocation! Here are some things to keep in mind:

- Practice *modernity* while remaining musical.
- Don't equate *modern* with *too much.*
- *Tell the story.*
- Who's modern? Not as many people as they think they are.
- Whatever style of music you're playing (modern, classic, neo, or retro), tonal and textural balance, and contrast ratios need to have an esthetic clarity and beauty.
- Don't be afraid to let the car slip into fifth gear and cruise for a minute. Simmer, swing, and make the music bubble and dance.

QUESTION: What's the best way to play your cymbals?

ANSWER: With love!

Seriously. Caress your cymbals when you crash them. In practical playing terms, this means to strike the cymbal with your stick at an angle or a glancing blow, versus a straight up-and-down hit. The glancing blow is also potentially less destructive to the cymbal's edge. The cymbal needs to be free to vibrate, so don't overtighten the wing nuts or use too many felt pads that might dampen the sound.

Also, don't grip your stick too tight. I allow my stick to vibrate whenever I play a cymbal, whether it's a crash, a ride pattern, or the hi-hat. All of my cymbals are *cymbals,* and because I play them with care and "lift" (pulling the sound from the instrument), they can all function as ride or crash cymbals.

Practice whole notes on the ride cymbal, and listen to the tone. Once you hear the sound you want, practice producing that consistent tone whenever you play. Learn how to swing softly, and other musicians will love you for it. I promise.

QUESTION: Is it okay to play jazz time on the hi-hat for more than just song intros and bass solos?

ANSWER: Yes, indeed. There are three ways to play time on the hi-hat:

1. Quarter notes and/or the ride pattern on closed hi-hats (Latin, pop, funk, and R&B drumming).

2. The jazz ride pattern played on *open* and *closed* hi-hats (opening the hi-hat before the pick-up to beats 3 and 1).

3. Open hi-hats (slightly touching one another) to create a simmering sizzle or buzz sound (hard rock players do this, too, but we're focusing on more finessed playing).

Remember that you're creating a world when you focus on the hi-hat, so take care not to disturb or interrupt the magic of that world. Anything and everything you add from the rest of the kit to the hi-hat time *must sound and feel good.* Focus on developing a simmering sound and control of the hi-hat.

Playing a closed hi-hat is easy. The *challenge* with playing an open hi-hat is the ability to be able to control the texture of the two cymbals being played together (however open or loose). The top cymbal thickness and weight, in addition to the context of the music, is a key factor in your decision-making vocabulary.

One of the best things I ever heard in my life was when drummer Joe LaBarbera began playing on the hi-hat at the start of a tenor solo by saxophonist Jimmy Greene. I expected Joe to move the time to the ride cymbal, but he accompanied Jimmy's sax solo on the hi-hat the entire time. It swung so much, and was so exciting. It was the musical equivalent of filmmaker Alfred Hitchcock's use of the "MacGuffin."

QUESTION: What's a "MacGuffin"?

ANSWER: *Film director Alfred Hitchcock coined the term "MacGuffin" when discussing the suspense techniques in his films.

A MacGuffin can be boiled down to one thing—nothing. Hitchcock over the years described the MacGuffin as a plot device (or gimmick) on which to hang the tension in a film, "the key element of any suspense story" (Gottlieb). Because Hitchcock lured the audience to such a high degree of sympathy for the characters through cinematic means, the reason behind their plight became irrelevant for the viewer. Something bad is happening to them, and it doesn't matter what. The MacGuffin's only purpose is to serve as a pivotal reason for the suspense to occur.

The MacGuffin is like a wild card that can be inserted to stand for anything. It can be something as vague as the "government secrets" in *North by Northwest* (1959), or the long, detailed weapons plans of Mr. Memory in *The 39 Steps* (1935). Or, it could be something simple like the dog blocking the stairway in *Strangers on a Train* (1951). Nobody cares about the dog. It's only there for one reason…suspense. It could have just as easily been a person, an alarm, a talking parrot, or a MacGuffin!

The hi-hat is more than a MacGuffin…but you get the idea.

This page written by/courtesy of Jeffrey Michael Bays.

CARE AND MAINTENANCE

Proper care, storage, and regular maintenance of your equipment will yield positive results for years to come.

Percussion Repair Kit (*Leave* Home Without It)

The following is a basic list of recommended tools and items that should be a part of your repair kit. We suggest you have these available at all times in your workshop. Items marked with an asterisk (*) should be carried with you whenever possible.

- Jeweler's screwdriver
- Straight screwdriver (medium)
- Phillips screwdriver (small, medium)
- Standard pliers
- Needle-nose pliers (small)
- Flat file (small, smooth)
- A set of hex-key wrenches
- *Drum key (and/or Torque key for marching drums)
- A multi-purpose gadget like the *Tama Multi Tool that contains all the small tools you might need when away from home
- Snare cord (to attach snare to strainer)
- Plastic strips (for snare units that don't use a snare cord)
- White lithium grease (Vaseline collects too much dust)
- Small can of silicone spray (Uline, 3M, WD-40, etc.)
- Cleaning rags
- Felt washers for cymbals and hi-hat
- Curved and straight metal washers for cymbals and hi-hat
- *Spare hi-hat clutch (make sure it fits all major hardware brands)
- *Plastic tubing to go over cymbal tilter posts or rod shafts (these can either be purchased or made at home from rubber tubing of various diameters).
- *Cymbal stand wingnuts

- An assortment of tension rods, washers, and double-claw hooks (for the bass drum)
- Extra drumheads
- *Extra sticks and brushes (We like to keep a spare stick bag in the car.)

Drumheads

Drumheads should be kept free from dirt and replaced when they become worn or broken. They may be cleaned with mild soap and water (though this is not common practice). Do not allow moisture to accumulate between the edge of the head and the counterhoop.

PROBLEM: I've pitted my drumhead, there's a dent in it, and I don't have a spare head.

TRICK: *Very carefully* apply heat to the dent by using the flame from a lighter. Do not do this in any space where an open flame might be hazardous! Take care, as well, not to burn a hole in your drumhead. This is a desperate (and temporary) measure, but it works and has gotten me out of a jam on more than one occasion.

TIP: *Keep spare heads on hand whenever possible.*

Drum Shells

Regular cleaning of your drums will help prolong their beauty and tone. Wood and pearl finishes may be cleaned with a damp cloth and mild soap; furniture polish may also be applied to wood finishes, if desired. Shells should be checked periodically for cracks.

Cymbals

Only clean your cymbals if you are more concerned with how they look rather than how they sound.

Fingerprints and dirt can be removed by using a solution of mild liquid dish detergent and warm water. Most cymbal manufacturers market specially formulated cymbal-cleaning products as well. If further cleaning becomes necessary, there are a number of nonabrasive commercial cleansers available on the market.

Never use steel wool, wire brushes, or any other abrasive cleanser. If a cymbal is exceptionally old and dirty, a stiff fiber brush may be used. Never use an electric buffing device, as the heat generated will alter a cymbal's temper, making it vulnerable to cracking.

Cymbal felts and plastic sleeves on cymbal stands should be checked on a regular basis to make sure that the cymbal is not making contact with the stand, which will not only restrict the cymbal's sound, but may also cause the cymbal to crack. To lessen or eliminate a rattle, try varying the relative lengths of the cymbal stand's tubing.

QUESTION: How do I remove dried duct tape residue from my cymbals and stands?

ANSWER #1: Invest in a bottle of Goo Gone.

ANSWER #2: Don't put duct tape on your cymbals or stands to begin with.

Repairing Cymbal Cracks

Even with proper care and maintenance, cymbals can still develop cracks. If a crack occurs, it must be eliminated as soon as possible because eventually the smallest nick will develop into a large crack.

For cracks that start from the outer edge and move inward, an eighth-inch hole may be drilled just ahead of the crack (*diagram A*). For cracks that appear horizontally across the bow of the cymbal, an eighth-inch hole should be drilled on both ends of the crack (*diagram A*).

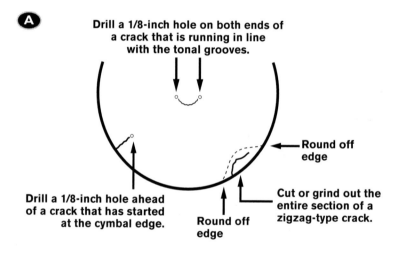

A

Drill a 1/8-inch hole on both ends of
a crack that is running in line
with the tonal grooves.

Round off
edge

Drill a 1/8-inch hole ahead
of a crack that has started
at the cymbal edge.

Round off
edge

Cut or grind out the
entire section of a
zigzag-type crack.

Cracks up to about one-half inch that appear on the edge of the cymbal can be ground out (*diagram B*).

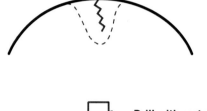

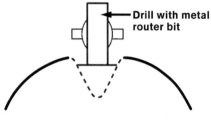

Drill with metal router bit

Never attempt to braze or weld cymbals, as the heat will cause irreversible damage.

REMEMBER: *These techniques have been proven to be successful in stopping cracks from spreading, but there is no guarantee they will work in all cases, or indefinitely.*

QUESTION: Should I spend my life looking for a cymbal that sounds like Tony Williams's ride on those incredible recordings he did with Miles Davis?

The surprise answer is "no." Legend has it that the actual ride cymbal Tony played on "Nefertiti" is nothing like what our ears might expect. It was heavy, and not as mysterious or dark sounding as many a boutique cymbal maker would have you believe. The *real* answer is in the touch.

Drummers in the old days might have altered the sound of a ride cymbal using various materials. Adding more felt washers or tape to the cymbal stand would help them dry up the sound as much as possible. Making cracks in the cymbal was the final way to alter the cymbal's sound before it died. However, cymbals today are made much more consistently than they were back in the day. The problem I have with many of today's extra-dry boutique rides is that while they may sound cool up close, they will not sound like much of anything out in the audience. A cymbal needs ring and tone so it can project its sound into the club or concert hall.

ADVICE: *Don't go overboard with the use of dry- or dead-sounding cymbals. You won't be doing yourself or the music any favors. There is a wonderful variety of cymbal brands and designs/models to choose from. Whenever you play a cymbal in a store, etc., be sure to take your own drumsticks with you, and ask a drummer to play that cymbal while you listen to it from a distance.*

Hardware

Lugs should be checked to make sure they are tightly secured to the shell. Tension rods should be lubricated with white lithium grease or light machine oil. Bent or stripped lugs should be replaced. Moving parts, including the snare throw-off switch, bass drum pedal, and hi-hat pedal, should be lubricated once or twice a year with light machine oil. Metal shells and hoops may be cleaned with a damp cloth and/or metal polish. Broken snares, warped rims, and faulty strainers should be fixed or replaced immediately.

QUESTION: How can I get rid of dust in hard-to-reach places such as in-between the lugs, and under the foot pedals?

ANSWER: Use a can of compressed air.

Snare/Tom Protectors

These are a good idea if your snare drum and mounted tom are touching one another. There's no quicker way to damage the shell of a drum than to have a snare and tom bumping into each other during an entire performance or recording session of music making. You can also make a simple pad by using a bit of gaffer's tape with tissue paper, and assembling this improvised pad onto the rim of the snare (where contact might be made with the tom). Or, you can simply purchase a commercially made bumper.

Protecting Your Bass Drum Hoop

Several companies offer bass drum hoop protectors that fasten directly onto the hoop in order to prevent the attaching claw of the bass drum pedal from permanently scarring or disfiguring the bass drum hoop. You can also improvise one by using the cardboard wrapper your drumsticks come paired in, folding that onto the hoop, and positioning it between the hoop and the pedal claw. We saw this drumming "hack" on YouTube, and it's pretty clever.

Restoring Worn Hoops

Worn hoops can be restored easily by following the steps below.

1. If the hoop has a plastic inlay, cover it up with masking tape.

2. Using a medium-grit sand paper, sand down any rough spots created by the claw hooks or the bass drum pedal. It is not necessary to sand all the paint off.

3. Before paining the hoop, use a finer-grit sandpaper to produce a smooth finish.

4. Using a flat surface, wipe the hoop off with a tack cloth, and place it on top of a piece of cardboard or newspaper. You might consider raising the hoop off the ground with the use of three or four small woodblocks.

5. If the hoop is black, spray it lightly with a good, flat spray paint. Once it's dried, go back and spray it with a high-gloss paint.

6. When the hoop is completely dry, remove the masking tape covering the plastic inlay.

Repairing Bent Claw Hooks and "T" Handle Tension Rods

A bent claw hook can be repaired by clamping a 5/16" or 3/8" in diameter steel rod tightly in a vise, placing the claw hook over the clamped rod, and hammering it until the original shape has been obtained.

"T" rods can be straightened by attaching the shoulder tightly in a vice (do not clamp on the threads), and hammering lightly until the original shape has been obtained.

Eliminating Buzzes and Rattles

It's a good idea to periodically inspect your drumset, piece by piece, for any loose connections, rivets, etc. This will involve taking the drumheads off, checking *all* of the hardware mounted to the shell of each drum, as well as all cymbal and snare stands, tom holders, etc. The obvious culprits include:

- Two pieces of the drumset rubbing against or making contact with one another
- A loose wingnut or tension rod
- A loose screw inside a drum
- An improperly seated drumhead
- A bass drum pedal that needs adjusting
- A rattle coming from the inside of a lug casing

Sympathetic Snare Buzz

If your snare drum is buzzing too much when you're playing a rack tom (usually an adjacent mounted tom), experiment with either loosening the two tension rods of the bottom head on either side of the snare bed, and/or changing the tuning of the tom that's triggering the inordinate amount of snare buzz. Please note the use of the word "inordinate." A little snare buzz never killed anybody.

On the Road Again
Cases and Storage

When ordering or referring to drum cases, always refer to the size of the drum shell, and not its overall dimension (which includes the hoop and head mounted to the drum). Most drum-case manufacturers will compensate for the overall dimension and will usually refer to the size of the cases as drum-shell sizes. If in doubt, be sure to measure the size of your drums in relation to the interior dimensions of whatever bag or case you choose. There's no sense in having a drum rattling around inside a case that's too big, or exposing a drum to risk because it's too large for the case (which also makes getting your instrument in and out of the case completely inconvenient...in which case, forget it!).

When your drumset remains set up but is not being used, keep it covered with an old, but clean, sheet or blanket to protect it from dust and dirt.

When your drumset is not in use for longer periods of time, place the drums in cases, and store them where they are not subjected to either extreme cold or heat.

When transporting your drums and hardware, we strongly recommended you use any number of commercially available cases (either leather, canvas, nylon, or fiber) designed specifically for the storage and transport of drums and hardware. Beato, Ahead, Gator, and Protection Racket all make good bags. Hard-case companies include Humes & Berg, Gator, SKB, and Hard Case. While most companies specialize in molded-plastic case construction, Humes & Berg still offers cases made from "vulcanized fibre" (as in the old days).

QUESTION: What kind(s) of cases should I get for my drums?

ANSWER: First, here's a brilliant idea that my wife offered to me in the form of a question: "Why do drummers put all of their hardware into one large trap case? It's so heavy! Why not use two smaller trap cases instead?" Bingo.

Use two medium-sized rolling bags or hard cases designed for drumset hardware. Your back will thank you for it.

As far as protecting your drums in town and for local gigs, soft bags are fine. If you're planning on having someone else handle your drums for shipping or flying, etc., hard cases are a must. Some drummers like to pack their drums inside a protective bag and *then* into a hard case. Can't hurt, but it seems like a case of overkill to me (pun intended).

Cymbals should not be stored where they will be subjected to either extreme cold or heat, as a temporary loss of sound may occur until normal temperature has been restored.

When transporting cymbals, you may want to use a leather, canvas, or nylon padded bag made specifically for cymbals. There are also fiber or plastic cases specifically designed for cymbal transport.

Bass drum and trap cases sometimes have special compartments for cymbals. If more than one cymbal is being carried or stored in a single bag or case, padding could be used to separate the cymbals to prevent scratching.

MAINTAINING A HEALTHY LIFESTYLE
(YOU'RE ASKING US?)

Being healthy is not just about what you eat, but how you live. Making an effort to eat better and live a healthier life can make a huge difference in your energy, mood, and self-esteem. Here are some tips to keep you physically and mentally healthy while on the road.

- Don't drive long shifts (switch drivers more frequently). If going it alone, stop every two hours to stretch your legs and rest your eyes.
- Try to get some exercise by either walking, running, stretching, or doing yoga. When staying in hotels, use the pool.
- Party in moderation.
- Incorporate relaxation techniques such as deep breathing, focusing on the present, laughing out loud, listening to smooth music, being grateful, visualization, etc.
- Get as much sleep as you can.
- Maintain good relationships.
- Spend time alone by exploring a new city by foot, reading a book, eating at a different restaurant from your travel companions, meditating, etc.
- Distribute the duties amongst all band members.
- Stay hydrated throughout the day by drinking plenty of water.
- Use a hand sanitizer when soap and water aren't available.
- Eat right! Avoid eating too much fast food. Carry a small cooler filled with fresh fruit, dried fruit, trail mix, vegetables, protein bars, etc. Whatever you eat, chew well, and eat with a sense of gratitude. Think positively about the food you're putting into your body.
- I play best after I've had some protein.

CHALLENGE: Touring/traveling without your own drums

TIP: *Be open to all playing adventures, including playing on someone else's drumset.*

BACKGROUND: I've done a lot of traveling, often without the convenience of having my own drums on tour with me. As a rule, I will (most always) carry my own cymbals and stick bag with me wherever I go. If circumstances allow, I'll also travel with a favorite snare drum— maybe even a bass drum pedal.

Whatever the scenario, I find it most helpful to carry a small bag of essential parts with me. Aside from the parts included in the section called "Percussion Repair Kit," I also carry the following:

- A small piece of sandpaper for removing some of the coating from a brand new snare batter head (for playing brushes).
- A pencil and a Sharpie pen.
- If your carry bag has room, a roll of gaffer tape (not duct tape) is always handy.
- Most everyone has a smartphone, and so you'll be set with a functioning flashlight for dark stages (or while walking backstage), a metronome app, and a camera for still photos or videos of your gig or recording session!
- A universal tool with built-in pliers, screwdrivers, etc., is always handy, too. Some items can be safely checked when flying, so make sure you conform to all TSA requirements when packing your carry-on items.

If and when I'm sitting in on someone else's drums, I tend to "play it as it lies" (to quote from golfing lore, as well as Buddy Rich, who said the same thing to Roy Haynes when Roy sat down at Buddy's drums and moved towards changing something!). Not only does the "new" set-up offer an interesting challenge, it's also an opportunity to show respect to the drummer and his or her kit. Sit down and play!

The best travel advice I ever got: "Always be good to the people who handle your bags and your food."

The best encounters-with-authority advice I ever got: "Never challenge the authority of *anyone* wearing a uniform. Whether it's a police officer or a doorman, these people can often make your life either simple or miserable."

The best day-to-day life advice I ever got: always approach a closed door knob or handle with your fingers curled into a fist (not straightened out). That way, if the door opens suddenly, your fingers will not get injured.

QUESTION: When flying, should I use a trap case or a suitcase?

ANSWER: One of the biggest traveling challenges involves carrying as much baggage as you need without breaking your back, or the bank. The dimension of most trap cases exceeds airline regulations regarding size. Plus, musical equipment seems to be the target for unnecessarily rough treatment by some baggage handlers. So, an alternative solution to using a trap case would be to use a regular suitcase for the job. Trap cases were originally designed to carry a drummer's cymbals, snare drum, bass drum pedal, and some lightweight hardware. Since most drummers now carry their cymbals on-board or transport them in separate cases, a trap case is not really needed. If you choose an appropriately sized suitcase, you can fit a snare drum (in a bag or hard case), a pedal, a stick bag, an accessories pack, CDs, after-gig clothing, etc., and the airline will not treat the bag as a special item (oftentimes setting it aside where it might miss its flight). Plus, the dimensions meet airline specs. Get a rolling suitcase with a pull-out handle, and you'll be in business (even if you're sitting in economy). We suggest a 28" soft bag with a zippered top, plus two wheels and a pull-out handle.

THE BUSINESS OF MUSIC

Whether you're considering a written offer or having a verbal discussion, the devil can be in the details when it comes to negotiating a deal. For any written contract, you should seek qualified legal counsel and representation. I've tried to go it alone on some big deals and regretted it later.

If you're being asked to do a gig by, say, telephone or email, here's how to handle such discussions. First, always thank the musician or artist rep for the interest in having you join a particular project. Once I check the calendar and confirm my availability, I will then ask to listen to some of the project so I can confidently determine if I'm the "right" drummer for that project (this approach is more polite than saying, "I want to see if your music sucks or not before I say yes…"), unless I know the artist's work. Then, it's a matter of agreeing on the terms:

Fee

- Will you receive gross or net (after taxes) pay if the project is a foreign engagement?
- Does your fee represent a "favored-nations" status (i.e., is your offer no lower than anyone else's)?
- Manner and timing of payment? (Advance? Direct deposit? Check? Cash? Union or non-union?)
- Travel expenses and conditions (economy or business class)?
- Per Diem (a daily allowance for food and typical road expenses)?

Recording

- How many hours/how many songs?
- Audio/visual rights (video)?
- Do I get album credit?
- Can I thank or mention the companies of the products I endorse on the album?
- If I'm with another record label, do I need to get permission to appear on this album/label? (It depends on your contract with that other label—seek professional legal counsel.)

Be polite. Be prepared to say no if you don't like the offer. If someone really wants you, he or she will improve the offer…but you need to know that you're okay if you're not pursued.

Don't Be Afraid to Say No

My wife was on the phone once with a contractor about a recording project—an album I was not particularly keen on doing—so I slipped her a note suggesting she ask for "triple scale." The contractor reacted with horror and dismay, informing her, "That's more than we pay so and so," to which she replied, "I understand...um, would you like so and so's phone number? I have it right here..." The guy agreed to our fee request. Know your worth.

Otherwise, be humble and do the work, because it's always good to do the work. Experience is priceless!

With that being said, my professor at Indiana University (George Gaber) often counseled me on the *importance* of being able to say no. If a gig conflicts with an important family plan, say no to the gig and prioritize your family. If someone wants you, he or she will always call you again.

Maynard Ferguson's Rule on Charity

Trumpeter/bandleader Maynard Ferguson once told me, "If you finish a gig and the club owner or concert promoter cries the money blues to you, don't accept less than what was originally agreed upon. However, once you are paid in full, *then* you can return some of the cash back to the promoter or owner, and your generosity will be better remembered and appreciated."

To be honest, I've never tried this.

Endorsements and Music Industry Companies

QUESTION: How do I get an endorsement deal with a drum company?

ANSWER: By not asking for one!

This may seem counterintuitive, but the best way to receive something is to neither expect it nor ask for it. Certainly make yourself and your interest known, but the latter is best expressed by simply conveying your admiration for a brand. That may include a long history of using a particular product (or products) made by a company. A recommendation made by a currently endorsed artist doesn't hurt.

Unsolicited contacts and pitches made by drummers to companies usually end up in the trash, especially if they're expecting free gear out of the gate. By the way, most of the gear is not "free" in the sense that it's given to you and you own it. Technically, the equipment belongs to the manufacturer or music company distributing a company's products. With perishables like drumsticks and drumheads, this becomes a moot point, but the cymbals and drums I play? These belong to those companies; otherwise I am liable to pay taxes on the goods received (Yamaha, for example, provides 1099 statements to drummers using their products). Since they are treated as income, those items *do* belong to the drummers in the end. After playing on DW drums for a few years and then leaving the company, I returned the drums they had provided to me.

Let your music do the talking. "Talent will out," as the saying goes. Once a company becomes aware of you, what you can do, and the type of person you are, they will come to you. Obvious bit of advice: Don't act like a jerk.

General Business Etiquette and Strategies

Don't be a jerk. Oh! I already said that.

Behavior on and off the bandstand is less of a strategy and more of a way of life, to be honest. I'm not "nice" to someone because it might improve my chances of getting something. I'm "nice" because I like to be pleasant to people and to leave a room with more smiles rather than less. So, it's always good to be polite.

Here's an important concept to remember from the worlds of technology and business, known as "the failure of the last mile." Essentially, you do not want the end result of your hard work on a project to be remembered only for an unfortunate final word or impression that undoes all of the good will you've been building up by means of being polite, engaged, playing well, and so on. I've been guilty, or have fallen prey, to this on numerous occasions, and it's almost always avoidable. Take a deep breath, and think before you speak.

Be grateful for the opportunity, *any* opportunity to make music, and don't say anything stupid on your way out the door.

Otherwise, make certain that there are no misunderstandings on when and how you are to be paid for your work, and for what that work entails. Be a man or woman of your word. And make sure you get it in writing.

How Do You Work with a Difficult Band Member or Leader?

I've found myself in the hot seat over the years, working for various bandleaders (or under the baton of notoriously difficult conductors) who were *not* polite and were, on the contrary, demeaning and/or abusive. The question I always asked myself was, "Is there something I can learn from this ("this" meaning the person, band, or circumstance I was working with), and is it worth allowing it to play out? Most often the answer was yes, as in, "These people know a lot more about this stuff than I do, so I'm going to hang in there." Otherwise, I would not hesitate to call someone, *anyone*, out on rude or inappropriate behavior. However, this should be done with care and tact. My father taught me a valuable lesson when he advised, "You must always give something to someone before you attempt to take something else away." So, the obvious example is by beginning a conversation with a compliment and getting the other person to feel comfortable or, at least, not under attack. Gaining just a small amount of trust can really help level out the playing field so two people can then discuss a musical or personality issue without defensiveness or rancor.

No one plays badly on purpose, whether it's *you* or *the other*.

Music, like math, does not lie.

Strive for musical honesty, truth, and beauty. Be a diplomat, and know your worth.

How Do You Tell a Bandmate to Turn It Down (Play Softer), and/or Make Suggestions?

Getting a musician to turn down an amp or monitor can be one of *the* most difficult things to accomplish.

Here's our advice:

If you're sound checking, it's vital that you get the front-of-house PA turned *off* at some point so everyone can hear what the stage volume and balances are truly like.

The softer your stage volume, the better everything will sound out front. Period.

Someone needs to be the point person on stage regarding this, and so it might as well be the drummer. Exercise your rights and leadership, as well as your unique seat in the "dynamics control department." Softer stage volume gives the band someplace to go dynamically, and it will sound better out front.

Volume is very much like a stack of dominoes—as soon as one element gets too loud on-stage, everything will get out of whack pretty quickly.

Be polite (that, again), but firm.

If possible, record the music both on-stage, as well as from the front of the house (i.e., the audience's point of view). You'll either get confirmation of what you suspect you hear happening, *or* you'll be surprised to learn that it actually sounds okay out front (or, horrors, that it's the drums that are too loud!).

The music does not lie. Sounds are not false, either…unless a sound person makes it so.

Here's one handy way to deal with bringing up a musical problem with a colleague, as illustrated by two contrasting approaches:

APPROACH #1: "I don't like what you're doing, so please change it." This will be met with resistance. After all, if someone said this to you, how would you feel?

APPROACH #2: "Hey, I apologize for the way that tune is feeling. I might be playing the wrong beat or hearing the music the wrong way (i.e., playing too on top of the beat, behind the beat, busy, or simple)." This will most often be met with a "thanks," plus a reassuring word that, no, you're not the only reason the song isn't working. *The other* will most likely add that he or she is having some sort of problem as well (personal or musical). As soon as someone feels safe in an encounter, the more willing the person is to admitting to possible shortcomings or a misunderstanding.

How Can Social Media Best Be Utilized?

Don't spend your life there. Maintain a healthy balance, and keep your social media posts short, entertaining, informative, and fun. Too much is a turn-off, so keep it short and sweet. A clever campaign of info combined with good sounds is always of interest to music lovers.

Try not to be tone-deaf when posting. The operative word here is *timing.* Be sensitive to world events (especially regarding the fate of others in the news).

If you're on Facebook, *band pages* are more effective than personal pages. Post your cat and dog videos on your personal page, and not on your band page. Twitter is useful. Instagram is fun, but only if you post stuff that sounds or looks cool. Obviously, YouTube works well for video.

Get yourself a website.

Don't believe everything you read on the Internet.

How Much Self-Promotion Is Too Much?

Here is where *the other* comes into play. Too many "I," "me," and "my" references are, frankly, boring. We shine the best light on ourselves when we praise others. Your music will speak loudest and best for you. With that being said, it's okay to let people know what you're doing, and it's okay to be proud of your accomplishments. But it's just like anything else in life. If you need to keep reminding people how good you are, then your music is not doing the job, and you'd be wise to get back into the practice room. "Music Speaks Louder Than Words."

Should I Attend Music Conventions?

Yes! Conventions, such as the Percussive Arts Society International Convention, the Jazz Education Network, and NAMM are excellent opportunities to not only see the latest and greatest instruments and gear, but to attend masterclasses, clinics, and concerts, and to network with other drummers and industry companies/leaders.

Is a College Degree Still Valuable?

- Yes! Many skills you acquire while earning a degree will be useful in other fields outside music.
- Pursue what you love, and not what you think will pay the most.
- If you're really passionate about a performance career, then go for it.
- Set a timeframe to reach your goal (five to seven years), and then move on.
- Have a plan B in place.

Alternate Careers in Music

Aside from pursuing a performance career, you have many other options available within the music industry. Some of the more popular career options include music publishing, music engraving, music retail, recording, music licensing, non-profit management within a music organization, personal assistant, copyediting, teaching, music therapy, composing/arranging, copyright administrator, music librarian, studio engineer, etc. Keep your options open! Music will always be in your life.

How Do I Submit a Manuscript for Publication Consideration?

- Make sure you're sending your manuscript to a music publisher.
- Do some research to see if there's something similar already on the market.
- If your subject matter is similar to something already on the market, explain how your book/approach is different.
- If you're unsure of what type of new books the publisher is looking for, contact them to ask.
- Include audio and/or video components with your book.
- Manuscripts should be addressed to the proper department and/or editor.
- If sending a printed copy for review, please include a self-addressed, stamped envelope for the manuscript's return. Manuscripts lacking return postage are usually discarded.
- Most of the major publishers ask that you allow approximately 8–12 weeks for a reply.
- Do not send your only copy to the publisher.
- Do not send your manuscript to a publisher if it's currently being reviewed by another publisher.
- Submissions should be original material.

PRACTICE TIPS TO MAKE THE MOST OF YOUR DRUMMING

QUESTION: What's the best way to practice?

ANSWER: For starters, you can think of practicing in two ways: one, to get as much playing time under your belt as possible, and, two, to focus on specific items or to practice with intent.

Practicing for practicing's sake will help you build endurance and strengthen some coordinative motor skills, but the downside is that you're most often playing what your hands and feet already know… *unless* you use this "free" time to truly pay attention to your rhythmic accuracy and consistency in execution. In other words, you should be able to practice what the music tells you to practice, and it's important to develop your ability to receive this feedback. That said, I find it most productive to practice specific things on the kit. And, if anything is presenting a challenge, I will steadfastly practice at a slow tempo, removing one or two "voices" (limbs) from the pattern until I can convince my brain and body that I can put everything together…and then I will increase the tempo until I have mastered what I have intended to learn.

Most drummers tend to practice the same things at the same tempos, over and over. And they practice what they know. I like to practice what I don't know. A journal helps me keep track of what I've worked on. If I hit a wall? I stop, take a break, and move on to something else for a change of pace. I can and will return to the challenge that was frustrating me with a clear mind and spirit; I enjoy the best practice success this way. I also concentrate when I practice in this manner. It is possible to accomplish much more in twenty minutes of concentrated practice time than jamming for two hours on the kit.

A mirror or video device is essential. Not only can you listen back to what you're playing (checking for dynamic balance, for example), you can play along with yourself to see and feel how the other musicians on the bandstand hear your drumming. This is a real ear-opener.

Unintentional cheating of the beat, etc., will immediately become apparent. The mirror or video will also reveal how much you are *externalizing* the beat (in the unintentional movement of your arms, legs, or head and neck) versus *internalizing* the beat and playing with the most control. The time is inside you, not in your raised forearm or bouncing leg. Put the movement into the music and not into your limbs.

QUESTION: Should I practice trades (4s, 8s, choruses)?

OLD ANSWER: Nah.

NEW ANSWER: Great idea—yes!

The old me used to think practicing solos and short trades was akin to cheating, feeling it was best left to spontaneous creativity. The new me (albeit an older me) now thinks that practicing such things is a good idea, because it increases our vocabulary and comfort level when being put on the spot or in the spotlight.

Here's one way to do it. First, make sure you practice trades at different tempos, and not just the one tempo you like to practice everything at. Next, start each set of 4s with the same two-bar statement, and then come up with as many different second-half "exit strategies" as you can. Once you've explored your creativity, do the opposite and reuse an effective or cool release or exit while coming up with new first-half intros. *Then*, practice complete 4s. You'll find that your confidence *and* creativity are increased in this manner.

A little discipline here and there will always work wonders for your drumming.

More Practice Tips

- Make sure your equipment is working for you and not against you. If you're experiencing pain while practicing/playing, look into the reason why and make the necessary fixes and/or adjustments.

- Spend time warming up at the beginning of each practice session to get the blood flowing and the body functioning smoothly and efficiently. Nonmusical warm-ups may include walking, running, or a variety of calisthenics.

- One of the most important roles of a drummer is to keep good time. Learning to practice with either a metronome (preferably one with a headphone output), a drum machine, or a computer with music-sequencing software will help you to achieve this.

- Start slowly. Practice each rhythm or exercise at a comfortable, consistent tempo before increasing the speed.

- Master the awkward and uncomfortable, and make music out of *everything.*

- Count aloud, and either clap or sing each rhythm before playing. Don't move on until you can play what you're practicing at an equal volume and tempo throughout.

- Maintain a relaxed feel while playing, and breathe normally (breathing and relaxation are very crucial elements of drumming).

- Listen to the sound you're getting, and strive to get the best tone from your drums and cymbals. It's not just mechanics. It's *tone.* Practice *touch* (I like to practice whole notes on the ride cymbal, which has contributed to the development of my cymbal touch and sound).

- Strive for proper balance. Are all the notes even and in consistent time? Are the parts of the drumset balanced dynamically?

- As you practice, use a mirror to observe your hands, arms, legs, feet, stick height, and posture.

- Sing or tap the rhythms first before attempting to play them.
- Try to look for any bad habits (your teacher or your own observations should point these out).
- Focus! When you're concentrating fully, things become more ingrained in your mind, making them easier to recall later.
- Experiment with rhythms and patterns that you create.
- Set new goals for yourself.
- Consistent practice is important in order to keep your body in good condition and to get the most from your practice sessions.
- Actively listen to a variety of musical styles, as this is one of the best learning tools available.
- If you don't have a band to play with regularly, use a play-along app or tracks.
- Keep a practice diary or log, and annotate or chronicle what you work on each day, and at which tempos.
- Always practice and play musically.
- Record yourself.
- Reward yourself!
- Enjoy practicing. Playing drums is fun, and regular practice sessions will make you a better player.

Cool Warm-Ups

There is much to be said for the melding of the mind and body when
we first encounter our instrument each day–a philosophy of biome-
chanics where the Zen rubber meets the road, as it were. We are
taught that "practice makes perfect," and that every practice routine
should include a warm-up session. But how many of us diligently
warm up before practicing? How often do we sit down to play a
concert or recording session without doing any sort of warm-up?
One thing we do know is that the older we get, the more helpful and
important warming up becomes. This is true for any instrumentalist,
and certainly for percussionists (jazz, rock, funk, pop, or classical).

The first thing I do when I arrive at my practice studio, or a dressing
room on tour, is to set up a practice pad on a snare stand, and take
out my Vic Firth SD1 general purpose sticks (these sticks are slightly "heftier" than my drumset sticks, and are balanced in weight and
tone). Once I'm set up and seated, I pay attention to my posture. I
then begin playing the same warm-up exercise I've been doing ever
since it was shown to me by Professor George Gaber at a summer
music camp back in 1966! Beginning with the right hand, I play
eight strokes, followed by eight strokes with the left; then seven (R),
seven (L), six (R), six (L), five (R), five (L), and so on. It looks like this:

8	7	6	5	4	3	2	1	2	3	4	5	6	7	8
R	R	R	R	R	R	R	R	R	R	R	R	R	R	R
L	L	L	L	L	L	L	L	L	L	L	L	L	L	L

The warm-up can be played either un-accented or with an accent at the beginning of each hand's new number. You can also play these in unison (without flams!).

SUGGESTION: *Begin slowly at a moderate dynamic level. The idea is to start relaxed and to gauge your hands' condition. Check your stick height, rebound, angles, etc. Whether you play matched or traditional grip, you should strive for an evenness in tone, volume, and the sticks' relationship to the playing surface. Have a specific tempo in mind when you start, and gradually increase your speed. Pay attention to how relaxed your arms, wrists, and fingers are.*

This exercise is valuable because it demands that you consistently pay attention to the number of strokes in each hand the entire time you're playing it. In this way, nothing becomes automatic. This should not be regarded as tedium. In fact, this should prove to be an enjoyable and essential part of each day.

I might practice this routine for five minutes or so, and then move on to playing open and closed double-stroke rolls. Again, I pay attention to stick height, rebound angle, and sound. Play these double strokes at various tempos and dynamics.

Next, try alternating between double strokes, single strokes, and paradiddles at a moderate tempo. It's important for all the strokes to sound as even (and seamless as you switch from one to the other) as possible:

**R R L L R R L L R R L L R R L L > R L R L R L R L R L R L R L R L >
R L R R L R L L R L R R L R L L R L R R L R L L > R L R L R L R L
R L R L R L R L > R R L L R R L L R R L L R R L L,** *etc.*

Here's an exercise I stumbled upon, more or less, just by going through various sticking combinations. After practicing some simple flams, I began playing the rudiment known as the flam accent:

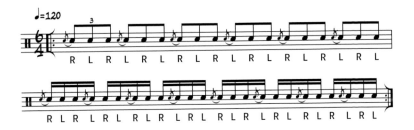

Here is a variation of the flam tap, called the Swiss army triplet, which comes to us courtesy of our drumming colleagues in Basel, Switzerland.

What I like about these versions of triplets is the bit of metric modulation that occurs as you switch between the (notated) triplets and the sixteenth notes. These triplet rudiments are also quite useful to play on the drumset.

I'll wrap up my warm-up routine with some simple L-R and R-L ruffs, along with some additional improvisations. All in all, I will generally spend anywhere between 10 to 15 minutes of private time between me, my hands, and my sticks. My muscles are relaxed, and the blood flow is good. When I go on-stage a short while later, I am confident and relaxed, and eager to sit at the drumset and play the concert.

The biomechanical benefits of warming up are obvious. It is the spiritual side, however, that might not be so apparent. The warm-up session is a sort of benediction to your playing day. It is quiet time alone, with the tools of your trade and the silent musical space around you. This is music waiting to happen. This is the time to breathe deeply, and to feel the expression of gratitude for what you're about to do. Your senses are now alert, and you can hear your sticks at work without the decibel din that a snare drum or full kit might bring. As you codify and confirm your sticking movements and execution, you are brought face to face with the very essence of being a drummer and musician. In essence, we think it in our minds, feel it in our souls, and say it with our sticks!

GLOSSARY OF WORDS YOU SHOULD KNOW

accent (>): Play the note with a strong attack (relative to the current dynamic level; see *sfz* (sforzando).

attack: The manner in which a sound begins.

balance: Occurs when performers adjust their volume so all players in the ensemble can be heard.

bass drum pedal: A device clamped to the rim of the bass drum and operated by the foot.

batter head: The playing side of any drum.

bead (or *tip*): The end of the drumstick normally used to strike the drum or cymbal.

bearing edge: The outside circumference of the drum where the head meets the shell.

bell (or *dome*): The top (center) part of the cymbal.

b-flat: Anything that is plain or unremarkable, as in "That was a pretty B♭ sandwich."

bow (or *profile*): The area of the cymbal between the edge and the bell.

brushes: Devices made of wire or nylon, used to strike or sweep a drumhead or cymbal. Rüte or Blasticks are normally made of thin wooden dowels.

busy: When you're playing too much, you're playing "busy."

butt end: The end opposite the tip of a drumstick. Commonly used for playing heavy backbeats.

calfskin head: A skin of a calf stretched over a hoop and mounted on a drum. "Calfskin" can also be made of goat and other furry creatures (like kangaroo, believe it or not).

cases: Used to store and/or transport drums, cymbals, and accessories.

chick sound: The sound produced by the hi-hat cymbals when the foot pedal is pressed and the cymbals are brought together/closed.

choke: To strike a cymbal and then dampen it immediately, an effect most often used with a splash cymbal.

clamp: A device used to attach the bass drum pedal to the rim of the bass drum.

clave: The Spanish word for "key" or "clue," and the rhythmic map or compass for most Afro-Cuban and Afro-Cuban influenced music. 3-2 ("Bo Diddley" beat) and 2-3 ("Peanut Vendor") denote the accent scheme over two bars of music (a song will start on one or the other). Listen to the melody and it will guide you as to which direction the music should be played.

clockwise system: A method of tuning carried out by moving sequentially around the drum, as opposed to the cross-tension system.

clutch: A mounting bracket used to hold the top hi-hat cymbal to the rod of the hi-hat stand.

competing thrills: Playing for the audience, yourself, or the music?

counterhoop (or *rim*): Used to apply tension and hold the drumhead in place.

cradle: The top part of a snare stand that holds a drum.

crisp sound: Sharp, clean, and clear.

cross-tension system: A method of tuning carried out by moving cross-wise around the drum, as opposed to the clockwise system.

cymbal tilter screw (or *thumb screw*): Used to tilt a cymbal, or the bottom hi-hat cymbal that sits on the platform.

dampening (*muffling*): Used to eliminate the ringing produced from a cymbal, drum, etc.

dance: What the music should do.

dark sound: Possessing depth and richness. Not as bright as a bright sound, to state the obvious.

decay: The gradual fading out of a sound.

desky: The sound or impression of a mix move that sounds artificial (i.e., done by means of a move on the mixing board or "desk"). As in, "That sounds pretty desky."

dome (or *bell*): The top (center) part of the cymbal.

drumhead: The material (plastic or skin) stretched over one or both ends of a drum and struck with a hand, mallet, or stick.

drum key: A key used to tighten or loosen the tension rods for the purpose of tuning or removing drumheads.

drumstick: A stick used to strike a drum or cymbal, consisting of a tip (or bead), shoulder, shaft, and butt end.

drum throne: What a drummer sits on when playing.

dynamics: Varying degrees of volume.

edge: The outer part of the cymbal.

explosive sound: Giant and sudden.

fat (or "*phat*"): The feel of a groove that sits deep in the pocket of the beat.

fatter attack: Full and rich. And, generally, placed on the back side of the beat.

felt strip: A piece of material used to muffle the sound of a drum; may be placed behind both heads of the bass drum.

finger dampening: To stop a tone from resonating, gently touch the instrument with your fingers.

flesh hoop: A wooden or metal ring to which the drumhead is attached.

foot plate: A plate on which the foot operating the bass drum pedal or hi-hat pedal rests.

four free (or *eight free*): in the studio, the number of clicks you'll hear before the first measure of music.

free: To play outside agreed-upon boundaries, whether rhythmic, harmonic, or stylistic. Also, as in lunch.

harmonic overtones: High pitches, other than the fundamental pitch, that resonate after a drum or cymbal has been struck.

heel-toe technique: A technique of playing the bass drum and hi-hat by which the entire foot contacts the pedal.

hi-hat pedal: Operated by the foot; brings the hi-hat cymbals together when pressed.

hole-cutting template: A pattern or mold used as a guide for cutting a hole in the bass drum head.

horizontal: A legato manner of playing time and comping, generally more swinging than "vertical" (see *vertical*).

improvisation: Creating music as you play. Instant composition.

internal dampening knob: Mounted on the outside of the shell and attached to the *internal muffler*; when turned clockwise, the muffler presses against the batter head.

internal muffler: When pressed against the batter head, it absorbs some of the vibrations and eliminates the after-ring or resonance.

kick, or kick drum: Another name for the bass drum.

lugs: Attached to the side of the drum and used as receptacles for the tension rods.

mallets: Sticks with a yarn- or felt-covered ball at the end, used to strike a drum or produce suspended cymbal rolls.

matched grip: Both hands hold a drumstick or mallet in the same manner (generally, with palms down).

miscellaneous: Music-making that is unfocused, as in, "Man, that percussionist is playing some really miscellaneous stuff…"

muffle or muffler: A device used to absorb vibrations and eliminate after-ring.

muffling: A technique used to reduce head resonance, ring, or harmonic overtones.

muted: Softened or muffled.

neutral clef: Used by percussion instruments of indefinite pitch.

opaque drumhead: A nonclear drumhead.

open: When the length of a section or solo is indeterminate.

ostinato: An accompaniment pattern that is repeated.

phrase: A musical statement or idea.

pitch: The frequency of a note in terms of its highness or lowness.

pocket: Deep time, in which the music is sitting in the beat and not feeling hurried or rushed.

point: The tap of a brush beat.

point tuning: A means of checking to make sure the pitch is consistent all the way around the drum.

profile (or *bow*): The area of a cymbal between the edge and the bell.

punch: With a quick, sudden blow or attack.

resonance: A ringing or long decay.

rim (or *counterhoop*): Used to hold a drumhead in place.

rim shot: Produced by simultaneously hitting the rim and head of the drum with a drumstick.

ring: A resonant tone.

rod: A part of the hi-hat stand to which the top cymbal is attached via the clutch.

rudiments: A system of sticking combinations that can be applied to the drumset.

schmutz: A slight rallentando (rit., ritardando) or spreading of the beat prior to the final chord of a piece or section of music. As in, "Would you like me to put a little *schmutz* in before that last chord?"

seat: The piece of the hi-hat stand upon which the bottom cymbal sits.

setting the head: A procedure used to acclimate the head to the shell.

shaft: The middle part of a drumstick between the shoulder and the butt end. This also refers to the bass drum beater rod.

shell: The frame that supports all the other components of the drum.

shoulder: The area of a drumstick between the tip (bead) and the shaft.

snare head: The bottom head of a snare drum.

snare release (or *snare strainer*): Attached to the side of the snare drum, used to engage or disengage the snares from the snare head by means of a throw-off switch.

snares: Wire, nylon, cable, or gut strands stretched across the outside surface of the snare head.

snare strainer: See *snare release*.

sock cymbals: Another name for hi-hat cymbals.

spring tension adjustment screw or knob: Used to adjust the tension/resistance of the foot pedal.

spurs: Attached to each side of the bass drum to help keep the drum from tilting side to side or sliding forward.

stick bag: Used for the storage and transportation of sticks, brushes, and mallets.

stick shot: Produced by placing the tip of one stick on the drumhead and striking it in the middle with the other stick. Also known as a stick-on-stick shot.

straight eighths: Regular subdivisions that are counted and felt *vertically*, or up-and-down.

swung eighths: Legato and lilting eighth notes with an accent or emphasis on the off-beat; there can be a suggestion or outright playing of the triplet feel (often times, tempo dependent).

tension adjustment knob: Used to adjust the tension or pressure of the snares.

tension rod: Used to hold the counterhoops in place and adjust the tension of the drumhead.

throw-off switch: Used to engage or disengage the snares from the head.

timbre: Tone color or quality.

tip (or *bead*): The end of the drumstick normally used to strike the drum or cymbal.

toe technique: A technique for playing the hi-hat in which the heel is raised from the pedal while the ball of the foot is used to activate the hi-hat.

tom-tom mount: A device attached to the side of the tom-tom that secures it to the top of the bass drum.

tone control knob: Mounted on the outside of the shell of the snare drum (and some tom-toms) and attached to the internal muffler; when turned clockwise, the muffler presses against the batter head.

torque wrench: A type of drum key used to tune marching drums.

traditional grip: The right hand holds the stick with the palm down, while the left hand holds the stick with the palm up.

transparent: Clear

tuning: Changing or adjusting an instrument to sound at a specific pitch.

vertical: A choppy, up-and-down manner of playing time and comping, generally straight eighth in feel, and not as legato or swinging as horizontal (see *horizontal*).

vonce: A jazz slang word that can mean almost anything.

ACKNOWLEDGEMENTS

We would like to thank Bill Platt, Aaron Serfaty, Jake Reed, Rick Mattingly, Mark Connor and Nick Beecher, James Prinzi, Holly Fraser, and Raj Mallikarjuna for their feedback and support. The book is much better because of your input.

Peter would like to thank the following companies who have supported him over the years—Tama Drums, Zildjian Cymbals, Vic Firth Sticks, Remo Drumheads, Meinl Percussion, Shure Microphones, Protection Racket Bags, and Finale Music Notation Software. He also thanks all of his students at the Thornton School of Music at USC (University of Southern California) for keeping him on his toes.

Dave would like to thank Peter Erskine for his collaboration, friendship, support, and inspiration. He would also like to thank the following companies who have supported him over the years—Yamaha Drums, Sabian Cymbals, Vic Firth Sticks, Mike Balter Mallets, and Remo Drumheads.

SOURCES

Truffaut, François. *Hitchcock.* Revised Edition. New York, NY: Simon & Schuster, 1985.

Gottlieb, Sydney. *Hitchcock on Hitchcock: Selected Writings and Interviews.* Oakland, CA: University of California Press, 1997.

Condon, Paul and Sangster, Jim. *The Complete Hitchcock.* London: Virgin Books, 1999.

Erskine, Peter. *Drum Concepts & Techniques.* Milwaukee, WI: 21st Century Publications, 1987.

Black, Dave. *The Drummer's Toolkit.* Los Angeles, CA: Alfred Music, 2003.